HIT BY THE CUPID STICK

BRIMSTONE INC.

ABIGAIL OWEN

XOXO

Abigail Owe

This is a work of fiction. Names, characters, places, and incidents are either the product of the author's imagination or are used fictitiously, and any resemblance to actual persons living or dead, business establishments, events, or locales, is entirely coincidental.

Hit by the Cupid Stick

Cover Art by *Abigail Owen | Authors On A Dime, LLC*

DEDICATION

To My Awesome Nerds

HIT BY THE CUPID STICK

All's fair in love and...whatever this is.

This Valentine's Day, when a cupid accidentally shoots himself with his own arrow, he falls for a siren whose only job is to lure men to their deaths.

Charismatic and irresistibly fun, Chance Eroson is a cupid who gets a kick from pairing odd couples and being right about them. Used to getting his way, the only person who shuts him down is the siren who has ruined more than one of his pairings before they started. But his bigger problem is he wants her. He's always wanted her.

Elodie Sirenian uses her power for good, only hunting evil men. But after so long, and so many horrible people, her cynicism has settled deep inside. She can turn on the charm when she doesn't mean it, and they fall for it. Every single one. Every single time.

Except Chance. He's the only person—man or god—who has ever challenged her.

But a cupid's magic is temporary. There's no way a true love match is possible. Not this time.

CHAPTER 1

ELODIE IDLY SIPPED at the fluffy pink drink some man at the bar had sent to her in an unoriginal bid for her attention. Some Valentine's Day special with candy hearts floating in the frothy top. The holiday was only days away. She really was more of a whiskey girl, but if the poor shmuck wanted to pay for her drink, she wasn't going to argue.

The uber confident man, dressed to the nines in a three-piece power suit, hair perfectly styled, teeth perfectly white, flashed her a smile and lifted his own glass in her direction. She caught the blip of hesitation that matched his aura, so she threw him a bone and tipped her drink in thanks.

She did *not* smile. Smiling would be an invitation, and three-piece-suit guy wasn't her target.

The man next to him, however…

Dressed casually in threadbare jeans and a t-shirt that looked as if he'd slept in it, her prey ran his fingers through shaggy, dirty-blond hair that needed a cut. Not a single woman in here was giving him a second look. There was only one reason Elodie was.

That aura.

The colored haze floating around him was as clear to

Elodie as the crystals in her favorite bracelet. Not black, like many of the men she hunted, his was a muddy mix of brown, grey, orange, and red. Studying auras was like a siren's road map of the human soul, telling her the most important information of who and what a person was in that moment.

She'd never—not in her two hundred years, seen a mix of colors quite like this. Self-involvement. Hopelessness. Self-control. Aggression. And anger. Lots and lots of anger.

As a siren, her job was to lure unsuspecting men to their deaths.

It had taken her only a single kill, when she'd matured and the hunger of her inner monster had first come upon her, to realize that she couldn't do what she did to *good* men. But to men who deserved it? Violent men. Abusive men. Those who posed serious threats to women, children, or innocent animals... Yeah. She had no problem ridding the world of their kind.

Three-piece-suit tipped his glass again, like she hadn't seen him a second ago.

What Elodie wanted to do was roll her eyes. What she did was lift her left hand and point to the diamond ring winking on her fourth finger. The ring she'd just slipped on under the bar. The one she'd bought herself just to deal with crap like this.

Three-piece-suit shrugged like that wasn't a problem and she briefly toyed with the idea of teaching him a lesson, just a peek at her monster, before she dealt with muddy-aura-guy beside him. But the suit was harmless. His aura was almost entirely yellow. He wanted to be alpha, but he was more like a puppy dog panting for attention.

Give him a scrap and he'd never leave her alone. Deliberately she swiveled the stool, turning away.

"I hope you haven't set your heart on the one I'm after," a deep, annoyingly familiar voice teased from behind her. "Because I have dibs."

Chance Eroson.

A royal pain in Elodie's perfectly formed ass.

Elodie closed her eyes and reached for patience. Sirens were supposed to be known for that particular character trait, but she never had been like her sisters.

"Chance," she acknowledged, pasting an insincere smile to her lips as she faced him.

Even knowing what to expect, impressions still hit in rapid succession. Broad shoulders, trim hips, a face somewhere between rugged and boy-next-door with floppy sandy-colored hair that somehow still appeared styled, and laughing blue eyes. Always laughing, at least at her. Unlike that panting puppy at the bar, Chance wore his three-piece suit—the suit didn't wear him. The red tie was a nice, if obvious, touch given what he was and the upcoming holiday.

If sin had a face, it would look like Chance Eroson. The man was as handsome as they came. Then again, a cupid would be. A child of gods, and a god himself, if a minor one, the man was genetically blessed. Same as Elodie. Which should make her immune.

It didn't. Which was the most frustrating part.

Wanting him was a character flaw she hadn't ever given into. As long as she didn't count getting herself off to thoughts of him. Which Elodie didn't.

Worse, his aura was...nothing. No color surrounded him. She'd found the same to be true of any creatures gifted with extra-long life and supernatural powers. Dragon shifters, berserkers, demigods, witches, it didn't matter.

Did it bother her that she couldn't get a read on him?

Absolutely. But she'd never admit it to him the same way she'd never admit to wanting him.

He'd better not be after the guy she was hunting.

Since arriving in New York some hundred years ago, she and Chance had clashed every so often. Usually when he wanted to hook some couple up, shoot them full of arrows that would make them fuck like rabbits and fall in love, and she had to intervene. The last time, he'd almost convinced her that the man in question would let go of his evil thoughts, thoughts the guy had never acted, for the right woman. That she would give the man a better outlook on life. A better outlet for his kind of energy too.

Almost. That man's aura had told her a different story though.

Chance could have been right. People were capable of change. But that guy wasn't. He may not have acted on his thoughts, but he would. Eventually.

She'd made Chance see it her way in the end.

Luckily, they hadn't clashed over too many people. Normally, Chance got it right, as far as she could tell. Though the man seemed to get a thrill from successfully pairing odd couples no one else would have seen together. Chance was in it for the challenge. She was in it for the mission. Rid the world of people who would see it burn. That and to slake the thirst of her monster.

"Who are you after?" she asked. She even used a pleasant tone of voice.

He stepped in closer, spinning her stool so she faced the bar, then closer still. Not touching, but she could feel the heat of him, the length of him, at her back. He leaned down to put his lips to her ear. "Him," he said in a low voice.

It had been a long time since a simple whisper had turned her on. She saw the worst in men. Even if she didn't kill them, she could still read their auras. Their lust with no emotion. Their aggression. Their manipulation. All of which made it difficult to rev her engines. So the fact that her nipples tightened, pressing against the silk demi-cup of her bra was…distracting to say the least.

"That's not helpful," she said dryly. "As usual."

His chuckle didn't help the nipple situation any, sending a surge of warmth cascading through her.

"Three-piece suit." Chance picked up her glass. "The one who just bought you a drink. Although, if he has his eye on you, it might make my job matching him a tad more difficult."

Elodie's muscles unknotted slightly. At least she wasn't going to have to argue him out of this one.

"With who?" Curiosity popped the words out of her mouth before she could stop herself.

"Banana yellow shirt in the back corner."

She searched behind three-piece-suit and found the woman in question. Not only was the lady's shirt bright yellow, but so was her aura. Elodie smiled despite herself.

"I take it you approve?" he asked.

How did he know? He was standing behind her.

"Otherwise, you'd immediately argue."

How did he do that? She knew a cupid could read the minds of humans—helped with the job—but he couldn't do that to her or other supernaturals. But the laughter in his voice told her he'd still managed to read her reaction regardless, and knew she'd be irritated about it. He didn't know that the irritation was because it meant he knew her better than she wanted. Dangerous to let him that close.

"Stay very still," he said next.

Elodie frowned and started to turn, except a glittering golden bow and arrow appeared at her side, arrow already nocked.

He had to be joking. "Here?" she drawled. "You're going to shoot them in a busy bar? Really?"

"They're lined up perfectly. I couldn't have picked a better shot." His voice was harder now. Focused. Sexy. If that's how he sounded in bed...

She shook off the thought.

"Hurry up." She had her own job to deal with.

"You don't rush love, baby girl."

"Call me baby girl, again, lover," she snapped. "I dare you."

She wished she could see Chance's face, because she suspected he was grinning. That title had always bothered her. "You're right," he murmured. "Lover is much better."

Elodie gritted her teeth.

The glittering, magical bow raised above her shoulder. The humans wouldn't see a thing. Not even his posture. Glamour of the gods meant they'd see something else. Probably him just talking to her.

"Very, very still," Chance whispered.

Which was when she happened to shift her glance from three-piece-suit to muddy-aura-guy only to find his gaze trained directly on her. Eyes as dark as an oil slick glared with an intent that any human woman would have shivered at. But Elodie could see that damn aura.

Without thinking she gasped and straightened in her seat, jerking back at the same time.

She knocked right into Chance as he loosed his arrow. Instead of going through three-piece suit and toward banana yellow shirt, it went up, hit the mirrored ceiling, and ricocheted backward right at Elodie.

The moment seemed to move in slow motion, and yet too fast for her to react. The glittering arrow pierced right through her chest, but no pain bloomed with it. Instead the sensation was like warmth and happiness and a bolt of pleasure directly to every erogenous zone, all in one.

A grunt sounded behind her just as she spun. "I'm sorry. I—"

The arrow lodged in Chance's abdomen suddenly disappeared in a fall of gold glitter. Her gaze connected with the god of love, and in that instant, she knew. She knew he was the one. She knew she'd found her match. Someone who could walk beside her in life who would be her everything and she would be his. At the same time, she also knew she wanted to hike up the skirt of her dress, unzip his pants and straddle the man. Right here. Right now.

Chance stared right back at her, his face etched with a thousand different emotions.

"What just happened?" she managed to ask through stiff lips. She already knew. Gods above, she knew. She was just hoping he might tell her she was wrong. But he didn't.

They'd just been shot with his love arrow.

She knew how they worked, had even seen it first-hand a time or two. Those golden arrows were designed to pass through the first person struck so it could lodge in the second person, until their connection solidified when they locked eyes for the first time. Even if it was days or weeks later.

An irresistible, undeniable connection.

Which meant she and Chance were screwed.

CHAPTER 2

"Fuck," Chance muttered.

He curled his hands around the back of Elodie's seat, doing his damnedest not to reach for her. Not to claim those agonizingly perfect lips for his. Not to do a hell of a lot more than that.

"Tell me your arrows don't work on our kind," she said. Practically begged. The strain around her mouth told him she was just wishing out loud.

He didn't know why she bothered. Hells he could smell her arousal. Honeysuckle and the sweet musk of a turned-on woman.

"I'm afraid they do, lover."

How she managed to widen and narrow her eyes at the same time, he had no idea, but it was…adorable.

A word he'd always associated with this woman.

Which was ridiculous. Sirens were born and designed to lure men. They oozed sex. Elodie more than most, in his opinion. White-blond hair tumbling over her shoulders and down her back. Deep brown eyes that offset her hair, giving her a mysterious air. That smart mouth of hers that came up with zingers that made him want to laugh. A mind he knew was hidden under the looks. And lips that should be wrapped around…

Damn it.

The thing was…she was more than her thirst trap outer shell. Even if she didn't want others to see that, hiding behind her seductress persona. Surprisingly caring for an ancient monster. She was the only siren he'd ever known to deliberately target men who were just plain evil. A lesson he'd learned the hard way the first time they'd met. He'd wanted to match one of her targets with a woman who would soften him. But Elodie had fought him tooth and nail.

Not his finest moment.

That's when he'd first learned that his instincts about pairs weren't entirely infallible. But he'd added more research to how he selected couples since then. Did a lot more mind reading.

"So…" Elodie licked her lips, leaning closer, pupils dilated. "What happens now?"

Excellent question.

Given how hard he'd already been before the damn arrow struck, thanks to just whispering in her ear—a stupid move even at that moment—he was in trouble now. Except… except she was clearly struggling with the same reaction. And that was only possible if…

He trailed a finger down the side of her cheek, skin petal soft against his touch. She closed her eyes, leaning into him.

"You want me," he murmured, while trying not to show the awe that realization shot through him.

He'd thought he was alone in the wanting.

A small, angry spark lit her dark eyes, turning the flecks golden, and she straightened away from his touch, only to lean forward again. "Of course I do," she muttered haughtily, "you struck me with one of your arrows."

Did he tell her now that the level of desire, or connection

—everything the arrow did—only built on what was naturally there?

He didn't make his couples feel things that didn't already exist. People who didn't know each other or didn't have a spark of chemistry wouldn't react to each other at all. Definitely not like this. But the ones where desire had been simmering under the surface for a while went up in flames. The ones with true liking fell in love in a blink.

He smiled softly. "What happens now is up to you."

She frowned a little. "I don't—"

"We have some…time…before the effects wear off."

Her frown deepened. "It wears off?"

Chance nodded. "My job is just to get a couple…started. A basic catalyst. It's up to them after that."

"How long do we have?"

He shrugged. "Depends on the couple, so it's difficult to tell." If she took him up on what he was about to suggest, he was damn well hoping for days.

She crossed her legs. Rubbing them together in an unconscious gesture and he knew exactly why. Because her body needed the same thing his did. Release. Immediate release. And only release delivered at his hands.

"So, what is up to me exactly?" she demanded.

His siren was getting antsy.

"You have two choices. Go home and lock yourself away until this wears off. A few days at most. It will be uncomfortable, but you can do it."

"Uncomfortable how?"

He narrowed his eyes. She knew. She just didn't want to admit it. Chance leaned in, hands on the bar on either side of her, forming a cage of sorts. Lips to her ear. "Option 2," he said, letting the heaviness of need sink into his voice so that she couldn't mistake it. "We fuck. A lot."

She was already tense against him and yet trembling. Resisting so hard.

But he wasn't going to talk her into this. It had to be her decision.

Only…gods he wanted her. He'd always wanted her. But no way he was pressuring her. He wanted the woman in his bed willing, eager even.

"Okay." Her answer came in a whisper.

Not good enough. He shook his head. "No. You're going to have to tell me what you want. I need to be clear."

Doe brown eyes narrowed and darkened. He could see the competitive side of her reflected there. The side that liked to be in control. Then she stood up off her stool. Chance was tall, but Elodie was tiny, the top of her head only up to mis chest on him. No doubt another physical attribute that lured men. Human men needed to feel powerful, dominating.

The move pressed her up against him, even as he eased back slightly to give her space. She looked him dead in the eye. "I'll take fucking, please."

She grabbed her purse off the bar top, took him by the hand, and dragged him through the crowd, out the door, and into a waiting taxi.

"Where to?" the driver asked.

Elodie looked at Chance. "Your place."

He grinned. His place it was. For the fucking.

Valentine's just got a hell of a lot more interesting, and it had already been his favorite holiday.

CHAPTER 3

ELODIE TRIED NOT to think herself out of her decision all the way to Chance's apartment. It helped that he'd teased his hands up her thighs a tiny bit more with each passing block until he was so close to where she throbbed, but not close enough, that she wanted to drag the touch higher. Because she wanted this. Truly, she did.

Why not take advantage of this...situation...and just enjoy? No guilt and no strings. She had a "Get Out of Jail Free" card. Plus, she hadn't been kissed by a man she wanted in...well, she couldn't remember the last time. Her prey never got past the kissing and maybe heavy groping phases, so it had been even longer since she'd been good and fucked.

And Chance was...

A good man.

Deliberately, she pushed that aside. The arrow was inducing lust. This didn't have to do with who they were as people, but the fact that their bodies wanted each other. Right?

That's all it could be for her at least. No good man ever encountered the monster inside her and stuck around. Not that many had tried. Just two in her lifetime. Both a disaster.

So she'd enjoy the fucking and do her best to bring him equal pleasure. Something for them both to enjoy fondly.

And the sooner the better, because the way her clit was pulsing, she was already at the edge of an orgasm, just on the idea alone. It was taking every single vestige of self-control not to straddle the man. Or unzip his pants and suck his cock. Or drag his hand further up her skirt. Anything to relieve this throbbing need.

Which was why she didn't say a word until they were inside his apartment. She took a quick glance around, noting that it suited him. Not a huge space, but it was still a loft with terrific views, both modern and cozy with the current day blend of contemporary and traditional with exposed red brick and wood beams paired with blacks, leathers, glass, and chromes throughout.

It felt lived in. A real home.

He reached for her but she stepped back. "Ground rules…"

Chance crossed his arms, jaw flexing, and she almost smiled. At least she wasn't the only one whose body was going haywire.

"Go ahead," he said.

"This is about fucking. Mutual gratification until the effects of your arrow wear off."

He nodded.

"No feelings."

He paused this time, but eventually nodded. "Anything else?"

"Respect each other's boundaries. I'm not into pain, otherwise just about anything goes. I'll tell you if I don't like it. You do the same. Agreed?"

"Agreed." He grinned. "I don't mind a little pain though, if you're moved that way."

Her panties soaked at the sudden thought of biting him. Like she was a godsdamned werewolf or something.

"Noted." How that came out not strangled, she had no idea. "Just one other thing."

He waited patiently. Gaze intent on hers, color flaring over cheekbones the only sign that he was at the edge of his control. "What?"

"If I don't come in the next five minutes, I might explode—"

Elodie squealed as she found herself scooped up against a hard male chest and just as quickly deposited beside the couch.

"I prefer the bed," he muttered through teeth now clenched. "But we're not going to make it there."

In a blink he unzipped his pants and freed his cock, then jerked the short skirt of her dress up to her hips. "This first round is going to be…"

"Good. Hurry."

"Care about these?" He hooked a finger in the side of her panties.

Her hair tumbled about her shoulders at the shake of her head, and, in one jerk, he ripped them right off her. Then she didn't know if she moved or if he moved or both, but he was seated on the black leather couch and she was straddling him, sinking down over the hard, hot shaft of his cock. So wet that she slid to the base without having to work him in slowly.

They both groaned, and Chance's fingertips bit into the flesh at her hips. Using that grip as leverage, he thrust hard. Elodie whimpered and his gaze lifted to hers. A sudden sense of…connection…trapped her in that blue-eyed gaze.

"Chance?" she whispered. A quaver in her voice. Because connection was against the rules. And she'd set those rules because more than just sex scared the hells out of her.

The grin that curled his mouth was pure sin. Still using his grip on her, he thrust again, and she tipped her head back, eyes closed, ready to enjoy the ride. He impaled her over and over in rough, heavenly, rapid succession.

That tell-tale tingling took up at the base of her spine, but then he suddenly slowed himself down. Elodie moaned. Gods she'd been so close. She needed to come.

Opening her eyes to protest, the words lodged in her throat. Chance was staring down at their joined bodies, something akin to fascination etched across his features, stealing her own breath as he drew out the way he possessed her body in long, slow, torturous thrusts.

How did he know that drag against her made her wild? And he kept it up until she was whimpering.

"Please," she whispered.

"Don't wait on me."

Elodie buried her face in his neck and inhaled. Gods he smelled amazing. Like her favorite scents of orange and coffee. Masculine and yet so who he was, refreshing and charming and invigorating.

"Take what you need," he whispered, and let her hips go. Giving her full control.

She lifted herself up, shuddering at the slide of him inside her, then down. Then harder, drawing a satisfying grunt from him. A noise that set her off like a firecracker. Letting go of everything that might hold her back, she took as much as she gave. She took her own pleasure from his body, ruthlessly. But at the same time, based on the string of words pouring from him—encouragement, swears, and a lot of "that's right, fuck me hard"—she knew she was giving pleasure at the same time.

Why that made her own pleasure deepen, she didn't want to examine. This was just supposed to be fucking. But damn he felt amazing.

Her orgasm hit with no warning. No pretingling sensation like from earlier. Just building and pressure and penetration, and then throw her head back on a scream as pure sensation hijacked her system.

Sensation that didn't stop until he swelled inside her, shouting his own release, which tipped her over into a second orgasm. The first one hadn't stopped though, sensation layering on sensation in the best way.

By the time they both slowed and stilled, her body was slick with sweat and he was still buried inside her, semi-hard.

"Holy shit," he muttered into her shoulder.

Her thoughts exactly. That had been...intense. Almost brutally fast. And...she'd enjoyed every damn second.

Then he kissed that same spot on her shoulder in the sweetest way which sent her heart tumbling over.

On a frown, she levered off his lap. This was just fucking. Hearts should *not* be tumbling anywhere. Jerking her dress down, she didn't look at him until she'd arranged herself more modestly.

Only to find he hadn't moved an inch. His still-hard cock lay on his belly and he hadn't covered up. Instead, he was watching her with a mash-up of curiosity, amusement, and heat.

The heat sent a new wave of her own building inside her again. Not softly either. Elodie pressed her lips around a groan. "Are you already...?" His cock twitched, if anything hardening more, and her eyes widened. "I guess you are."

At least she wasn't going through this fuck-frenzy with someone who didn't have the same effect happening. That would have been embarrassing.

Chance grinned. "For some people, apparently the first few hours can be intense. I guess we're one of those lucky sets."

Lucky? She had no idea what to feel about that. She'd said no feelings. She'd had her heart shattered before. Thought she was in love and he loved her back. He'd gotten one look at her monster and ran. Feelings were dangerous.

So right now it was best to just focus on the physical.

Besides, this all had to be the arrow, right? Not real.

Without a word Elodie backed up a step and whipped her dress over her head, then took off her bra. Chance went so still where he reclined and yet his gaze could have scorched her, and her hands stilled, fumbled even.

He wasn't looking at her with that lust that her prey usually did. A reaction that had nothing to do with her as a person.

The look in his eyes was…Chance really wanted her.

Her.

And he did know her. Better than most, actually. He may not have seen her kill, but, otherwise, he knew her. But to him, she wasn't just some easy piece of ass or a one-night quickie. Not that there was anything wrong with that, if that's what both parties wanted. But so many centuries of only being looked at that way tended to make a girl jaded.

Forget her tricks and forget the fact that they both had to endure this because of that damn arrow. She would just let go and enjoy being touched and looked at like that.

And she'd do the same for him.

Smiling, she turned and put an extra sway in her hips as she walked straight to the floor-to ceiling-windows that looked out over the bright lights of the city that never sleeps. With the lights on in the apartment behind her, anyone could see inside. See her standing in only thigh-highs and heels.

She placed her hands on the glass and leaned over, spreading her legs wide, then glanced over her shoulder at Chance, who still hadn't moved, his chest rising and falling sharply with each intake of breath.

"Join me?" she asked, her voice sultry. Not because she forced it to be. It just came out that way. For him.

CHAPTER 4

HOLY HELLS. Elodie Sirenian was going to be the death of him.

But dying like this…what a way to go.

Chance was up off the couch and across the room to her, and his body was insisting that he bury himself balls deep inside her, but the smile she'd given him when he jumped up had been both teasing and pleased with herself.

Time for a little tit for tat now that they'd taken a bit of the edge off with that first round.

He placed one palm flat between her shoulder blades to hold her still. With the other, he traced the lines and curves of her, his touch a gentle brush that would both torment and titillate. He didn't go near a single erogenous zone though. Came close. Teased. But no direct contact.

Chance kept that up, and enjoyed every damn minute of it, until he had her trembling and frustrated as all get out. "Fuck me, damn you," she muttered.

"Not yet, lover."

Even if he was aching so hard his balls were drawing up inside him.

But he did let both hands wander, pressing himself

against her back and reaching around to cup her heavy breasts. Play with them. Roll her nipples until they were like pebbles, hard against his palms, then he pinched. Not hard. She'd said no pain.

Her scent wafted to him along with her whimper, and he allowed one hand to stray down to her damp curls, then lower still, slipping inside her. Hells, she was soaked for him, juices dripping down the insides of her thighs.

He pulled his fingers out and she whimpered at the loss, then her entire body jerked as he found that bundle of pure nerves and flicked it.

Her gasp hit him right in the gut.

So he flicked again.

And again, and again, and again, until, with a cry she pitched over into another orgasm, body shaking against his as it ripped through her. He had to hook his arm around her waist to hold her up as the waves crested. And as she came, he aligned his cock at her slick entrance, timing his thrusts with the shudders wracking her body.

He wasn't gentle either.

He knew, as wet as she was, and the way she'd taken him earlier, that he wouldn't hurt her. Her sweet pussy clamped so hard around his hard cock, it took all his self-control to keep from spilling his seed inside her right then.

Instead, he gathered her hair in a fist, using that to hold her steady, and slammed his body into hers. Once.

"Okay?" he asked.

"Yes," she was panting hard by now.

He reared back and slammed deep again, this position giving him a new angle. Turning her head with the grip he had on her hair, he smiled at the way she'd closed her eyes. He watched the side of her face as he did it again, power surging through him at the way her lips dropped open.

"Look at me, lover."

She turned her head a little more, eyes on his, and gods

she was the most gorgeous thing he'd ever seen. Pupils blown out and lips parted in bliss, totally enthralled in that sexual haze some women could get to. And *that* had nothing to do with the arrow.

This was entirely her and how she responded to his touch. To *his* godsdamned touch.

"Touch yourself while I fuck you," he demanded roughly.

She slipped her hand between her legs and, not taking her eyes from his, moaned at her own touch. He slammed into her and didn't stop, kept up that ruthless rhythm, holding off his own release, until with hardly a flutter of warning, she cried out, clamping down on him hard. Strangling his cock until he exploded inside her on a roar as her greedy body drained him.

He barely kept them both upright as she collapsed in his arms. Somehow, he managed to scoop her up and walk her through his apartment to his master bathroom. There, he undressed himself—hells, he hadn't even taken his pants off yet—then slipped her thigh high stockings and "fuck me" heels off. He managed to bundle her hair on top of her head and got them both under the spray of hot water in his shower.

Laying tiny kisses across her skin, he resisted enjoying another round. "Don't fall asleep on me," he whispered.

"Hmmm…" she hummed back, body pliable but eyes on him. Not with heat but curiosity.

Smiling that he could touch her this way, he gently cleaned them both up. She didn't say a word until he wrapped her in a fluffy towel. "That was…lovely."

Almost as if thanking him for treating her sweetly. What kind of men had she been with not to expect sweetness?

The same as the kind of women he'd been with probably. For a god of love, he'd struck out in that department. Too optimistic for some. Too sexual for others. Too a lot of things. But he'd always held out hope, even after two centuries.

"My pleasure," he murmured.

Her answering smile was entirely unguarded and sincere.

Chance knew, right in that moment, that he was in trouble. He'd agreed to no feelings, but he wanted more than a few days of fucking. He wanted way more. Hells, he'd always wanted more from Elodie, and he wasn't going to fuck up this opportunity. Given her skittishness, that was going to take some doing.

Somehow, he managed to keep it together. He dried himself off and took them through to his bedroom. Sliding between the cool sheets, he pulled an extra blanket over them both when she shivered, and wrapped her up in his arms. They needed to rest if they could. Given their start to how they were both reacting to his arrow, they probably wouldn't have long before they turned back on.

Next time he was going to show her slow and gentle. He had two days, three at most, to change her mind about the no feelings thing. He needed her to know this wasn't temporary, or just an easy flirt, that he was serious.

CHAPTER 5

THE LOW RUMBLING inside Elodie's head woke her. Her monster needed to feed. Last night she'd already been on edge, but not getting her prey made the need worse. If Elodie didn't get to feed in the next day or two, her monster would unleash without her control.

What if that happened with Chance? Gods, she couldn't risk it. Somehow, between blissful orgasms, she needed to get away and sate a different hunger.

That's how it was for sirens. Humans had two hungers— food and sex. Sirens dealt with a third. An insatiable hunger, feeding off the aura of the men she killed. A need that would never go away. She could never have normal. No relationship. No family. That she dreamed of more made her pretty fucked up. She'd never told her sisters, or anyone she knew, stuffing those dreams down in the dark hole inside her where her monster lived.

Chance knows, though, a small voice whispered.

He'd once told her that she deserved more from the world, and the side of her that wanted more had almost listened. But Chance didn't know everything. And asking him to tie himself to what she was…that wasn't fair. Not to a man like him. One who actually seemed to believe in love, and romance, and happy ever after.

So she'd continue to ignore that want and make sure to feed her monster as soon as she got a chance.

Elodie blinked her eyes open in the morning light streaming in Chance's bedroom window. No blinds on the windows either, just like the living room. Was the man a voyeur or an exhibitionist or both?

Probably both. God of love and all that.

Nothing wrong with it. She'd been an exhibitionist herself last night, letting him fuck her against that window was about the hottest thing she'd ever done. In two hundred years on this earth, that was saying a lot.

She waited for that small warming sensation that was a warning they were about to need another round to sate their need. But it didn't come as it had every other time either of them had woken up all night long. Maybe they were through the worst of the effects?

A sudden weight around her heart at that thought sent a surge of surprise through her. She might keep her emotions on lockdown—hard to turn into the monster she became to kill her victims otherwise—but she knew what disappointment felt like. And she was honest enough with herself to acknowledge that's exactly what this heaviness was.

Disappointment.

Part of her didn't want this to end. Chance had been...a revelation. In the best of ways. Both so gentle he'd brought tears to her eyes and rough but always checking to make sure there was no pain involved. He'd bathed her, fed her dinner, kissed her like he'd meant it.

He could become an addiction if she let him. Good thing she'd been clear about no feelings. She'd hate it if she broke his heart.

Needing to move, Elodie stretched, then caught herself smiling at the small twinges in her muscles. Muscles that hadn't been used that way in far too long. With only a little rest in between, they'd gone at it most of the night. She'd lost count of how many times.

He'd reach for her. She'd reach for him. It didn't matter. It just felt damn good.

And for someone who'd just had a marathon bout of sex and very little sleep in between, she should be exhausted, but instead she was…exhilarated. Invigorated.

She hadn't felt this good in ages.

All because of Chance Eroson's magic cock…and hands… and mouth.

And arrow, a small voice reminded her.

She'd found herself forgetting more than once through the night that this wasn't real. This was just a contrived fuck fest to force a connection to manifest.

"What's the frown for?" he rumbled against her in a sleep-laden voice.

Elodie slowly rolled over to find him facing her, watching her with an arrested expression. How had he known she was frowning?

Deliberately she schooled her features so he couldn't read any more. "Nothing," she murmured. "Except, I'm hungry."

Chance winced. "I don't have a lot to eat in here. What I scrounged up for dinner was about it."

"That's okay. I saw a bagel place downstairs. They any good?"

That grin of his might be her undoing. Charm and eagerness and sex all rolled into a lopsided smile. "I'll go grab us some."

He hopped out of the bed, and she gave herself permission to thoroughly enjoy the view. Gods really did come in the most beautiful packages, especially Chance. Heat surged into her cheeks at the sight of her own teeth mark on his ass. Good heavens, what had she been thinking, biting him like that? Marking him like he was hers.

He'd told her he liked a little pain. The memory of what he'd done after that bite sent another fresh surge of heat through her.

What was wrong with her, blushing like a virgin on her wedding night?

"Any flavor of bagel or schmear?" he asked as he dressed.

"Plain bagel with strawberry."

He paused with his t-shirt halfway on. Then shook his head and laughed.

"What?" She pushed up to sitting, holding the sheet over her curves.

"You're just kind of adorable, is all." He shrugged the shirt the rest of the way on and was out the door before she could respond. She was still absorbing that anyway.

Adorable? No one called her that.

Sexy. Mysterious. Fuckable. Bitch. All that, of course. But adorable? She wasn't the type.

Another glow of warmth settled in her chest that he thought of her that way. One that she pushed back down with determination. Rather than lay here and get trapped in unhealthy wishes, she got up. Her dress was not an option, but neither was eating a bagel in the nude. Not if she wanted to finish the meal. So she went through Chance's closest and pulled out a black button-down shirt, rolling up the sleeves. In his drawers she found he wore boxer briefs and found a pair still in the wrapping. So she put those on.

Then she explored. The cozy, lived-in vibe she'd gotten last night made sense now that she had a chance to look around. His life was on display for anyone who looked. Pictures of him in places all over the world and knickknacks from the same spots. Books bound beautifully in leather, many first editions, and yet they'd clearly been read. Books on all sorts of subjects—the classics, biographies, histories. Like her he'd lived the last few centuries of history and knew creatures much older who could give first-hand accounts, but he read histories anyway.

She kept wandering, enjoying his choices of art and décor. A massive tome bound in red took pride of place on the desk in the spare bedroom and, curious, she opened it, only to still. Each page were pictures and descriptions dedicated to the couples he'd joined together. Not just his initial research. He'd kept up with them afterwards. There were even wedding announcements and birth announcements from newspapers.

He wasn't just in it for the game. "You really care," she whispered.

A knock sounded at the door and, with a jerk, she straightened guiltily. Only he didn't come in, he knocked again at the front door. With a little frown she made her way to it. "Did you forget something and lock yourself out?" she called as she tugged it open.

A rough hand clamped around the back of her neck and another, holding a sickly-sweet smelling rag, clamped over her mouth and nose. Then blackness took her under.

But not before she recognized his face…and his aura.

CHAPTER 6

THE BAGELS LAY by the elevator where he'd dropped them. Scattered and schmear face down, and he didn't give a shit.

Chance had come upstairs from getting them, humming. Actually fucking humming like he was happy. He should be more worried, because convincing Elodie to give him a proper shot after the arrow wore off was going to be quite the task. The woman had turned shutting off her emotions into an artform.

Even this morning, just asking her about why she was frowning, and suddenly all trace of emotion was wiped away, giving him nothing. Not an inch. Every time in the past he thought she'd softened, she'd shut back down and walled up her defenses.

How did he get her to drop them permanently?

On that thought, the elevator car had dinged and doors slid open. One step into the hallway he'd seen his neighbor on the floor beside Elodie's unconscious form.

Fear wasn't an emotion he dealt with often. Not in his line of work or his life in general. It hit so hard he grunted, the taste of it metallic in his mouth. Chance had dropped the bagels and run to her side, on his knees. "What happened?" he demanded.

He'd known Roger for ten years. Ever since he'd moved in. The man was built like a pro wrestler and worked as a bouncer. He was also a total teddy bear on the inside unless someone was hurting women, animals, or kids. Then he turned scary.

Kind of like Elodie that way.

"Some asshole had a rag to her mouth. I think he knocked her out. He was trying to drag her to the elevator. I yelled. He left her and ran for the stairs."

A rage that he wasn't even aware he could possess shot through Chance like an inferno. What the fuck?

Part of him wanted to hunt down the motherfucker and rip his head from his body. Again, something cupids didn't ever think, let alone do. But Elodie moaned softly. She needed him.

Chance would have more questions later, but for now, he framed Elodie's face with his hands. "Elodie?" Nothing. "Ellie. Baby girl, please wake up."

A tiny flutter to her eyes sent a spike of relief straight through his heart.

"That's it, gorgeous," he encouraged. "Eyes on me."

She gave the tiniest, most precious frown. "Is it time to fuck some more?"

Beside him, Roger coughed. Chance shrugged, too focused on the woman lying in the hall outside his apartment to care what his neighbor thought about that. "No, Ellie. It's time for you to wake up."

The eye fluttering turned to blinking until she finally managed to force her eyes all the way open, frowning at him, then at Roger. "Um? Hi?" she said to his neighbor.

Roger grinned, though the expression was more relieved than amused. "You're all right now," he said, softly, giving her leg an awkward pat. "The guy ran off."

"Guy?" Her frown turned hazy and then she stiffened, jacking up to sitting so fast she bonked heads with Chance.

Rubbing at his temple, he sat back. "Do you remember anything?" he asked.

"Some of it. Someone knocked at your door. I thought you forgot your keys…but it was…" Her eyes widened and she opened her mouth. Then she glanced at Roger and appeared to reconsider. "Do you mind if we go inside?" she asked Chance. "I'm feeling a bit woozy."

Chance didn't even ask. He just scooped her up, the same way he had last night for much more pleasurable reasons and walked them inside to the couch where he laid her down. Only to wince when Roger followed a second later with the bag of bagels he must've gathered off the floor and got an eyeful of Elodie's clothes strewn across the otherwise immaculate room.

That's what he got for being a neat freak.

"You should call the police," Roger said.

"Already handled, my friend," Chance assured him. Not that he would. Elodie wouldn't want that. Gods and sirens didn't involve human authorities.

"Right." Roger deposited the bagels on the kitchen island before quickly backing out.

The door was closed before either he or Elodie could say anything. "Who was that?" she asked finally.

Chance blew out a long breath. "Give me a second here," he said. "You scared the piss out of me, Elodie." His heart was still pounding.

"I—"

"I'm going to have nightmares about you lying there unconscious like that for the next decade."

Her eyes went wide. "I'm okay. Really."

"Yeah." Color was coming back into her cheeks. Thank the gods for that. She was also staring at him like she might bolt. All that talk of being scared for her was probably against her no feelings rules. Chance cleared his throat and answered her earlier question. "That was my neighbor, Roger. He scared away the guy who knocked you out."

She stared back at him a beat. "I would think so. He's built like a freight train."

Chance forced an easy grin. "Yeah."

"Nice aura though," she murmured, more to herself.

Normally he'd ask. Ever since the first time she'd put a stop to one of his pairings, citing the man in question's aura, he'd been fascinated. But at the moment, Chance was still barely keeping his shit together and trying not to show her.

The ripping that dickhead's head off was still top of his options. But he didn't want to leave her. Maybe he'd call in a favor and set a werewolf on the guy's ass instead. Those scary fuckers could hunt. Or, even better, a dragon shifter. Nothing came back from dragon fire.

"What do you remember?" he asked to stem the flow of bloodthirsty thoughts.

She grimaced. "The guy from last night."

The guy? "Three-piece-suit?" he asked. No way. That guy was puppy-dog harmless.

Elodie shook her head. "The guy I was after. Seated next to three-piece-suit. You know...how I bumped you and that's why your arrow hit us?"

Even in the midst of concern, he couldn't stop the grin from spreading over his features. "It rings a bell."

A flare of color surged into her cheeks, and a shot of answering need about took him to his knees. He'd made her blush several times in the night, and it was becoming an obsession. Because sirens did not blush. Not with the way they used their bodies as bait. Then again, Elodie had always been different.

Or different for him? His chest tightened at the thought.

"Anyway," she gave him a tiny shake of her head. "I moved because I glanced across the bar and caught him staring."

Chance frowned. "I'd think you'd be used to staring by now," he said, trying to work through why that was a bad thing. She hadn't just moved, now that he thought about it. She'd jumped. "And if he was who you were after, why was that a problem?"

"Because of the *way* he was looking at me."

Cold ran through his veins. "What way?"

"Like he wanted to kill me."

Well…fuck.

"Had you seen him before?"

She shook her head. Then paused. "Though…I guess he was a little familiar. Maybe I've seen him around? At another bar?"

Her preferred hunting grounds.

"I guess that makes sense." Chance didn't want to scare her but… "He followed you here."

"I know," she whispered. Then reached up to cup his face. "You really were worried about me?"

He startled. Did she really have to ask? Trying not to scare her off with feelings, he reined in his response. "Of course."

Her lips trembled just slightly before she leaned up and pressed them to his. Not a gesture driven by desire, but one that was sweet. An acknowledgment. "Thank you for that," she whispered against his lips. "But I do have some defensive skills."

He'd never asked how she killed her targets. Never seen. But he'd heard. Sirens were formidable monsters, apparently. It was so hard to picture her as anything but who she was right now. Casually gorgeous in his shirt, hair a rumpled mess around her face, not a lick of make-up, and softer. More herself, he hoped.

"I know." He tucked a strand of hair behind her ear. "But you have to be awake for that, right? What if he'd dragged your unconscious body out of here and killed you before you woke up?"

She wrinkled her nose. "Good point."

"I have them every so often." He grimaced. "But, even after the arrow wears off completely, I think it would be safer if you kept me around until we figure out what he wants with you."

Cupids were lovers, not fighters, but he was still a god. He had other tricks. Options. And no one was hurting Elodie. Not while he had breath in his body.

Her lips pressed together. "We'll see."

Which meant no. But he could be stubborn too. "Yes. We will. If something happened to you, I would never forgive myself."

After widening in surprise, her dark eyes softened, and his insides turned to mush at the sight.

"Well, for now, he's gone. I'll make a few calls to my sisters, and a friend who has…connections, and see what they can dig up."

He'd make some calls himself. Later. When she couldn't listen in.

He had a different problem now, though. The thing was, sitting here with Elodie's body pressed against him, her lush scent around him, her lips kissing his in the sweetest way only moments ago, and the danger run off for now and the effects of the arrow still sharpening every sense, every reaction to her… He shifted uncomfortably. "I brought bagels," he latched onto the first thing that wasn't fucking he could think of. "Some might still be edible."

Elodie smiled, the light in her eyes knowing. "I know I just got almost kidnapped, but is it terrible if I say I'm not hungry for bagels quite yet?" she whispered.

Part of him wanted to jump in and take her up on the implied offer. But… "How hard did you hit your head?"

She blinked, then laughed. "Not hard enough to make me horny."

Oh. Good. "I just…want to make sure you're okay."

The way she bit her lip…fuck. "I'm okay." Her eyes turned liquid, hot and slumberous. "I could be a whole lot better."

Thank the gods. "I could help you with that," he whispered back. Then kissed her, long and soft and slow. The way he'd been wanting to for ages.

CHAPTER 7

"TEA?"

Elodie heard Chance's question over the hairdryer he'd let her borrow. "Getting over being attacked" sex had led to "against the wall sex" had led to "shower sex." Now—after managing to place a few calls about her attack first, particularly to her friend Delilah—she sat on a teak stool at his vanity, wearing his shirt and boxers, drying her hair with his dryer.

And it felt…nice.

As long as she ignored the monster and the gnawing hunger inside her. The kind food wouldn't satisfy, only aura.

She clicked the dryer off. "What?"

Only he didn't answer. Instead, he stood staring at her with a crooked smile. "You look good in here Elodie. In my place."

No feelings, she tried to remind herself. But gods she wanted to agree. Wanted it to mean something.

But getting involved wasn't fair to either of them. Eventually he wouldn't be able to handle her reality.

The last time she'd gotten feelings involved with a man, he'd eventually become sickened by what she did. By the blood and the killing. She'd tried to hide it, but even his imagination was too much for him. The demigod before that had grown jealous over her occupation and the men she was hunting. Even though she'd been killing those men. He had tried to have Zeus punish her for "cheating." That had been a whole thing. The gods' punishments weren't exactly level-headed or fair. Besides which, she'd done *nothing* wrong by their laws.

So she stuffed her own wants away and wrinkled her nose at Chance. "What did you ask a second ago?"

He seemed to have to shake himself out of his own head. "I asked if you wanted tea."

Did he know tea was one of her favorite things? Or had she landed on the only man in America who liked tea? "Yes. But I'd better make it."

Really, she only said it to poke at him a bit. They were both competitive by nature. Getting Chance to lose his cool had become a bit of a game through the years. One he recip-rocated.

He didn't disappoint now. In typical Chance-fashion, he lifted a single eyebrow. "Seriously?"

Elodie shrugged, then pulled out her sexiest pout. "I make Very. Good. Tea."

He crossed his arms, unaffected, which she found oddly sexy. "I tell you what. You make some and I'll make some and then we'll compare."

She shrugged. "I'll win, but if your ego can handle it, okay."

She flicked the dryer back on and turned her back on him. Ten minutes later, she found him in the kitchen with all sorts of tea paraphernalia scattered across his counter. So he really did like tea. That was so...cute. She slowed, taking in the scene.

If anyone had told her this was how she'd be spending a Sunday, she would have laughed herself hoarse.

He grinned at her expression. "You expected me to just have tea bags, didn't you?"

"Something like that," she murmured. "So how is this little competition going to go?"

"Easy. We both make two cups the way we like best, then try both."

Suddenly an entire lifetime with this man laid itself out in her mind. Eons of…this. Of silly fun. Of just hanging out and laughing and competing with each other.

Elodie blinked all those images—so real and vibrant and distracting—away with effort.

They were supposed to be keeping this light. No mental pictures of forever. Those were definitely not a good idea.

"I propose a small twist," she said. Anything to bring this weekend back to what it was supposed to be.

Chance waved for her to share.

"We don't do this at the same time. The person not making tea gets to distract the one making…any way they wish."

A near feral light entered his eyes, pushing the laughter out even as his mouth twitched. "Any way I wish?"

"That's what I said."

"Then you better go first making the tea."

Her eyebrows lifted. "Why's that?"

"Because after I suck your clit until you come all over my face, you won't be able to stand up."

Despite having orgasmed three times already today, her body flushed with immediate heat that pooled at her core. Even so, she laughed, shaking her head. "Competitive at everything, huh?"

"With you?" He beckoned with a crooked finger. "That's half the fun."

He saw their encounters as fun, too? She hadn't realized. If anything she figured he found her annoying, always pushing and prickly and poking at his abilities. Why did the fact that he found it fun instead make her want to melt? Just a little.

"Drop your drawers, and come here," he said in a voice gone total alpha, rough and commanding.

And damned if her independent, jaded heart didn't give a flying fuck. She even smiled, putting every watt of siren behind the look, and enjoying his dazed blink. "Uh-uh. I'm not making the distracting easy for you."

Almost an hour later, they both sat on the kitchen floor, backs to the island cabinets, panting, sated, and damned if his tea wasn't better than hers.

"You'll have to tell me how you do that." She dropped her head back against the cabinet.

"Well, I like to start by tongue fucking you before I—" He cut off with a grunt when her elbow connected with his ribs, then chuckled, the sound floating right into her.

"I meant the tea," she huffed. Well...fake huffed.

"Ah. I have an even better concoction that I break out on Valentine's Day if you'd like to try..." He trailed off. Maybe because she tensed beside him hard enough that even the most oblivious of humans would have noticed. "I guess you're busy on that day," he said.

It was as good an excuse as any. Way better than forgetting for a moment that this would be over in a day or two. She wouldn't still be here on Valentine's Day. "The human holidays are always busy for me, but especially that one. The worst of the derelicts tend to up their game on Valentine's."

"As a god of love, that hurts."

She closed her eyes. "Stalkers, in particular. Those horrible excuses for humans take things to an entirely new level that day. Besides, even for humans who are good people, it's become a farce of a holiday anyway, don't you think?" Then winced, because she'd let some of the bitterness that had built inside her over two centuries leak out. In front of Chance.

He sighed. "I'll admit, humans, as usual, have taken a lovely idea and turned it into something ridiculous, overblown, or even hurtful."

She turned her head, expecting him to be teasing her, but found only sincerity staring back at her from blue eyes that reminded her of the ocean where she'd been born. "Really?"

He turned so that he was facing her more directly, as if he wanted her to believe him. "Really."

He meant it. Even her siren sisters never agreed with her when she got drunk enough to let this opinion out. To them, Valentine's was practically a siren holiday. Prime hunting grounds.

"What do you think Valentine's should be about?" she asked softly. And probably she should have regretted asking. Getting to know each other was against the rules. It invited feelings. But she wanted to know.

"Let's put aside the history of the date—which, by the way, didn't originate with my father, Eros, but started as a fertility holiday. In more recent centuries, it has become a day to exchange tokens of affection with lovers and friends alike, so it makes sense that the gods of love would be involved."

Elodie couldn't help herself. "I do love those chubby cherubs on the cards—"

That earned her a scowl. "Take it back."

She laughed, then leaned forward and kissed him better. "I think humans had to stick to cherubs. The reality of you would have blown them away."

He grunted, but a secret smile tipped the corners of his mouth up. "Anyway, while I think people should tell or show loved ones they love them every day, and not be forced into it, celebrating love is important. Without love…the world becomes selfish, chaotic, myopic. Love is what keeps us from becoming…"

Chance trailed off and Elodie's heart pinched, because she knew what he'd kept himself from saying.

"Monsters?" she prodded, unflinching. She knew what she was.

His hand tightened on hers. "*You* are not a monster, Elodie."

"I know." Chance was one of the few, other than her sisters, who knew that she chose to only target those who deserved death. "But it's not because I love."

He frowned. "It isn't?"

Was he going to hate her for this? "It's because I can't stand other monsters."

She waited for him to frown, or argue, or point out the logic problem. Because, technically, her sisters fell into that category and she didn't kill them.

"I'm sorry you see yourself that way," he said in a low voice that unclenched something inside her. "I don't."

She wanted to believe him. Believe the light in his eyes that told her he saw her. *Her.* Not the outer trappings of a siren or some dangerous creature to avoid. But the heart of her. Someone torn by what she was, by her family, and by her own moral compass.

She wanted to believe in him…but hope was a dangerous thing.

Besides, how could a cupid and a siren ever hope for more than just good sex. Their lots in life were too distant. Too at odds.

She needed to lighten things up. Fast. "You know I've never had a Valentine?" She smiled. "I don't think I'd want all the hoopla. Diamonds or cards or flowers."

Seeming to sense her need to take a step back, Chance flashed his easy smile. One she thought, just for a second, was tinged with disappointment. But she didn't let herself ask. "What would you want?" he asked.

"I don't know." She shrugged. "Something easy. A night

where I could be in pajamas, get takeout, put on a movie, maybe eat chocolates in front of a cozy fire, and just enjoy my…somebody."

The way he was searching her gaze, Elodie couldn't tell if he liked that or thought she was being silly.

Chance sighed. "I want—"

Her cell phone went off. Elodie knew that ring tone. The person calling would only be doing so for one reason. They had information on her attacker.

CHAPTER 8

TURNED out Elodie's contact wanted to meet in person. When she told Chance that, he thought it didn't bode well, but he didn't know this Delilah woman. Unfortunately, meeting in person meant getting them both cleaned up—again—and dropping by Elodie's place so she could dress.

Her apartment alone was…a revelation.

Cold. But cold on purpose, was his impression. Immaculate furniture in whites that he was afraid to sit on. Generic art that was more about colors and shapes, but nothing identifiable. No personal items anywhere. Not even in the kitchen, which had zero appliances beyond the basic fridge and stove. Not even a microwave.

Not even tea paraphernalia that he could see, and he knew she liked that.

Looking around, a weight pressed down on him. He would find living here isolating, and it seemed so far afield from Elodie. The real Elodie whom he liked to think he'd gotten glimpses of from time to time, and even more since that arrow struck them. *That* woman was warm, and funny, and teasing.

And lonely.

Anyone who surrounded themselves in impersonal nothing had to be lonely.

"Let me just swap out purses," she was saying as she emerged from her bedroom.

Chance had only ever bumped into her out on the prowl in dresses that were classy but clearly part of the image—body hugging, showing cleavage, abs, legs, or some combination, hair teased out, and full make up on.

Which meant that Elodie dressed in jeans and a hoodie with sequins and the words "Women rule the galaxy" was cause for pause. Because damned if minimal makeup, hair up in a messy bun, slouchy clothes, and converse sneakers wasn't about the sexiest thing he'd ever seen on her.

"Star Wars or Star Trek?" It just popped out.

She glanced down at her top and smiled. "Both actually. I know that's a cardinal sin, but I'll fight anyone who tries to put me in a box. I have every right to love both Yoda and Spock."

Chance chuckled. His siren was a closet geek, and he sort of loved that about her. "Fair enough. I'm all about Star Wars if you're wondering. Obi Wan is my hero."

"Killed by his padawan?" she mused as she moved items from her evening purse to a larger bag. "Seems an odd choice."

"The man *let* Vader kill him. For a reason. He's a bad ass."

Elodie laughed. "Well, come on, bad ass. My contact will be waiting."

The address she gave the cabbie had Chance raising his eyebrows in question, but it wasn't something to discuss with a human audience. Not until they were deposited on the steps of a slickly modern building. Having replaced whatever had been there before, it was surrounded by four and five story brick buildings lining the street all the way down. But this one was all glass and light and stuck out like a minotaur in a china shop.

No sign adorned it to indicate what it was. Chance already knew.

"The Covens Syndicate?" he asked in a low voice.

Gods didn't have much to do with the witches and warlocks of the world for the most part. In general, they had little need for the magic wielders' gifts. Or judgments. Or very human ways of making things more complicated than they needed to be.

"Just the eastern North American headquarters," Elodie murmured back. "My contact's mate is—"

The door was opened by a woman probably nearing her late sixties who wore her steel-gray hair severely scraped back from her face, not a strand out of place. Her face matched the hair. Where had she come from anyway? He should have seen her through the glass walls.

"Ms. Sirenian," the woman murmured, and waved them inside.

"Nice to see you, Agnes," Elodie said as she passed the woman, who didn't react at all. Not a smile or a nod or any indication she'd heard.

"This way." Inside, Agnes led them around the foyer desk to a back hallway and finally to what appeared to be a small, single office.

The second he saw who was waiting for them, Chance jerked to a halt. Just because gods didn't interact much with the wiccan world, didn't mean they were ignorant of the magical leaders. And this man was *the* leader.

Elodie's contact was the head warlock himself? No wonder he'd gotten her answers far faster than any of Chance's contacts.

Chance received a nod of greeting.

"Sorry," Elodie said. "Chance, I'd like to introduce you to Alasdair Blakesley, head of the Covens Syndicate."

Any person who headed the group that governed all mages worldwide at such a young age had to be incredibly powerful. Early to mid-thirties at most and imposing with raven-black hair and blue eyes that seemed to stray to the woman he stood beside more often than not.

"And this is his mate, and my friend, Delilah."

Wait. Her contact was Alasdair Blakesley's mate?

Chance studied the woman as he shook her hand. She was dressed in a pristine, deep purple pantsuit, and her black hair was pinned in an elegant chignon at the nape of her neck. Her demeanor and Alasdair's position might cause one to assume she was the less dangerous of the two, but the way the hairs on the back of his neck rose at her touch, if anything, he got the impression Delilah was the more powerful. And not necessarily a witch.

He didn't ask what she was. That question was considered rude. He just waited.

"Delilah owns and runs Brimstone Inc."

Now *that* he'd heard of.

"The firm dedicated to helping supernatural creatures with all sorts of problems," he said, eyeing the woman with a thousand questions. "Castor Dioskouri is a friend. He has only good things to say about your services."

Alasdair's smile was full of pride for his mate. Delilah's own smile, which had been warm, disappeared behind a frown. "You have your memory?"

His memory? What was she talking about?

Before he could ask, she waved a hand. "Sorry. I get visions from time to time, and I had one where we met. In that vision, you'd recently been shot by one of your own arrows and it gave you amnesia."

Amnesia? That was known to happen, but a rare reaction. And, until Elodie, he'd never been hit with an arrow. He'd remember. "I did get shot recently," was all he said, and tried very hard not to glance at Elodie.

"Hmmm…" Delilah mused. "The vision must have been

off because of this." She smoothed a hand over her still flat belly. "This isn't the first vision that's gone slightly awry."

Elodie gasped. "You're pregnant?"

At Delilah's glowing nod, she hugged her friend. Other than these last days together, this was the biggest show of emotion he'd ever seen from his siren.

Did Elodie want children? See herself ever settling down?

"Thank you," Delilah said. Then focused on Elodie. "But we're here for a reason. The man who tried to take you is named Cretan Pasiphe."

Beside him, Elodie tensed. "Pasiphe?"

"Is that familiar?" Delilah asked, exchanging a glance with Alasdair.

"A year ago, I hunted and killed a man named Tavros Pasiphe." She shook her head. "I thought that guy in the bar looked familiar, but I hadn't gotten his name yet."

Just like her tensing, he caught the slight vibration of her shudder. Without thought, he put a hand to her lower back. Thankfully, she didn't seem to mind. Even leaning closer.

"I guess evil runs in the blood," she murmured, more to herself.

"Maybe," Chance admitted. He'd seen enough of humanity to believe that. "But evil is also a choice."

"There's more," Delilah warned. "We know that Tavros and Cretan were brothers. But they also aren't entirely human."

They both tensed at that.

There was no law or even understanding that supernaturals wouldn't kill each other. Hells, the dragon shifters had only just found peace after five-hundred years of strife and war. But...

"I knew Tavros was supernatural—though I didn't bother to find out what. But I didn't sense anything supernatural about Cretan," Elodie insisted. "I could see his aura. It was awful but looked human enough."

"I'm not surprised," Delilah said. "He's descended from a long, diluted line of minotaurs. More human than bull now. But he lives in a commune with many full-blooded cousins. And he wants vengeance for Tavros."

Well…fuck.

CHAPTER 9

ELODIE TOOK a deep breath as she walked into Chance's apartment.

Minotaurs.

Like wolf shifters descended from werewolves, the breed of half bull-half men had somewhere along the lines learned to shift at will, allowing them to blend in more easily among humans. Those creatures were notoriously bad tempered.

And I killed one.

Granted, a bad one. She'd broken no laws among her kind. The fact that they were half-human had to be why she'd been able to see their auras. That happened sometimes. But if Cretan was after her now, he wouldn't give up until she was dead. Stubborn was like a badge of honor to his kind.

Elodie was aware she was being quiet. Chance had kept shooting her searching glances all the way back to his place, which they didn't exactly decide to go to together, but somehow they'd ended up here anyway.

The arrow's power, while less potent than it had been, was still affecting them both. And honestly, she liked his place. It felt lived in. Homey. Welcoming.

A lot like the man himself. Depths to him that she hadn't

realized until now. Or maybe hadn't wanted to let herself realize.

She could make it maybe one more night before she'd be forced to feed. Hopefully, that would be enough time for Delilah to track down Cretan and eliminate this little problem.

In the elevator on the way up, Chance had hooked his pinkie into hers, and it hadn't made her want to pull away. Yes, she'd wanted to jump his bones, but she'd also wanted to cuddle into him.

Danger warnings that these were emotions and feelings she shouldn't lean into were going off like fireworks in her head, but she ignored them all. For once.

"I ordered take-out from my favorite Nepalese restaurant to be delivered," Chance murmured to the top of her head. She vaguely remembered him making a call in the cab but hadn't been paying attention.

"I hope you don't mind?"

She shook her head. "I love Nepalese."

A huff of a laugh escaped him and she glanced up. "What?"

"The minotaur thing threw you hard, didn't it?"

How could he tell? "What makes you say that?"

"Because you don't let anyone do anything for you, let alone pick what food you'll eat."

He wasn't wrong. And, yes, she was distracted in several different ways. But that didn't take away from the fact that, for some reason, she didn't mind when Chance took care of her like this.

Danger. Big fucking emotional danger alert.

She pushed that voice deep where she couldn't hear it anymore. Or maybe the power of the arrow did. She was tired of listening to that voice. She flopped onto his worn leather couch and tucked her legs up under her, staring out the floor-to-ceiling windows over the New York skyline.

Mid-February it still got dark fairly early and the lights were more brilliant up here, where she could look across the city.

And he let her just sit in silence. Oddly comfortable silence.

Eventually, Chance dropped down on the matching leather ottoman in front of her, elbows on his knees. "What do you want to do about this minotaur?" The doorbell chimed and he sighed. "Save that thought."

She didn't plan to share that thought. This was *her* fight, not Chance's. She was also perfectly capable. Hells, between her and a minotaur, she was the bigger monster. Now that she was on her guard, Cretan wouldn't stand a chance.

Rather than make her get up and go eat in the kitchenette, Chance brought the bags of terrific smelling food over to her, sat where he'd been a second ago, and started pulling stuff out. Elodie hadn't realized how ravenous she was until this moment, and tucked in.

She was slurping up a long noodle of lafhing when Chance chuckled. Glancing up mid-slurp, she found him watching her with a grin. "What?" she said around the food.

"I knew the face you presented to the world wasn't the real you. Now I have proof."

Elodie wrinkled her nose. Because she got what he was saying. She never let anyone see her like this. Never. "What made you think that before?"

Was she slipping up in her duties?

"Because I do the same thing." He shrugged as if this wasn't a personal revelation. "Enough that I recognize a mask when I see one." He eyed her suspiciously. "Before all this, I bet you assumed I was just some kind of slick charmer with a magical bow and arrow who took nothing all that seriously?"

Elodie shook her head. "I've knocked the charm right off you a time or two." Seen the man underneath. Hells, his

49

letting her see his apartment showed her the man underneath. A man she liked.

He grinned at that. "I still say that the couple you stopped me from shooting would have worked. He hadn't acted on any of the impulses you could see. She would have given him the happiness he needed to resist. I get this gut sense."

She knew all about gut senses. "I'm sure you were right," she acknowledged.

Chance leaned forward, hand to his ear. "What was that? I don't think I heard you."

She rolled her eyes at his antics, lips twitching. "But…"

"There's always a *but* with you."

True. "But that small possibility that you were wrong, given what I could see…it wasn't worth the risk."

His gaze turned serious. "I know."

She stared. "You do?"

He'd argued tooth and nail with her each of those times, before stomping away in a manly huff.

"I researched them. Followed them. Bad guys. Every single one."

"Is that why you quit arguing with me any other time I stopped you?"

"Yeah." She thought he might leave it at that, but after a long beat, his lips quirked. "Thankfully, my job isn't finding fated mates, though I stumble across them from time to time. If you had tried to stop me pairing one of those rare couples, I would have argued harder. But my job is just to help humans get out of their own damn way and find someone who would make them feel…good or whole or seen."

Elodie melted a little, remembering the red book in his office. Chance was a good man. No doubt about it. "You want to know how I know the charm is a show?" She pointed her fork at him. "You care too much about your pairings working out for that to be all you are. So I've known this about you since the first time we met."

He hadn't turned on the lights in here, but even in the dim, the color flaring up his neck and into his face was unmistakable. "Chance Eroson...did I make you blush?"

"No," he grumped.

Elodie chuckled. "I did." And it was adorable.

He only grunted by way of reply. "So...we're both masters of illusion."

Something she'd always recognized. While she didn't exactly understand his faith in love, she still respected the talent and skill that went into the illusion of who he was and the practice of what he did. And she could see mutual admiration in his eyes as he gazed at her, or even when he'd fought with her. Chance, maybe more than anyone, understood the games she played to lure men. Hell, he might even play those games better than she did, because her heart wasn't in it, while she suspected he did everything with his heart. He was...a kindred. The other side of her coin.

She liked him.

If she was being honest, she'd always liked him.

"I still don't get that whole love thing," she murmured. "Humans are terrible."

Chance's smile widened. "Are you teasing me, Elodie Sirenian?"

"Maybe." Just a little.

He chuckled and the sound shot warmth straight through her to her heart. Direct hit.

THEY'D FALLEN asleep on the couch.

Chance stared down at the tangle of Elodie's white-blond hair as he blinked himself awake. After eating, they'd done mundane things like clean up and brush their teeth and dress for the night. The woman sprawled on top of him hadn't emerged in sexy lingerie, but in a t-shirt and baggy pajama pants with her hair piled in a messy bun on top of her head.

He'd give anything to see her like that every single night.

It also, of course, meant he hadn't been able to keep his hands off her. Forget the effects of his arrow. This was entirely her effect on him. Period. So he'd bent her over the arm of his couch and fucked her until she'd screamed her pleasure. Then cuddled her in his arms and they'd talked. About anything. About nothing at all.

Hell, they'd both fallen asleep watching a Hallmark Valentine's romance movie—Chance's pick, not Elodie's. He grinned at how she stopped complaining when he started his "good parts" watching technique.

"What are you doing?" she'd asked when he started fast forwarding.

"Skipping to the good parts."

"The romance?"

"Exactly."

She'd rolled her eyes, muttering something about cupids and their appalling belief in love. But she'd been invested in the couple on screen by the end.

"That's why the newest Pride and Prejudice is the best one," Chance had told her. "Because they skipped to the good parts."

"How about a nice, grisly murder mystery next?" she'd countered.

Which had made him laugh. She made him laugh a lot, actually.

He glanced at the still glowing TV and the clock on the wall beside it. Three in the morning. Damn. They'd gotten little to no sleep last night. He should either stay here and go back to sleep or get them into bed. But hands off. They needed rest.

The crick in his neck from sleeping semi-sitting with her on top of him told him the bed was better. Carefully, he scooped Elodie up in his arms and managed to get them both off the couch and to his room without her making a sound.

He slipped her between the sheets and stared at the woman in his bed, her pale hair spread like a halo on his pillow, her curves outlined by the sheet and blanket. She looked...right...in his bed. Like she belonged there.

Tempting to wake her up and bury his hard cock in her warmth, make her want to stay. Make her want to belong here. But the shadows under her eyes told him she needed rest more than fucking right now, so he resisted.

As he moved to his side of the bed, she frowned. "Chance?" she murmured his name a little fretfully, her hand smoothing over the bed covers like she was searching for him.

For *him*.

In that exact moment, he gave her his heart.

Nothing to do with his arrow. His magic didn't make love happen where none existed.

"Chance?" she murmured again, eyelids fluttering open.

He moved between the sheets and scooped her against him. "I'm here."

Elodie relaxed instantly, warm and womanly against him. "I thought you'd left me."

Had she been left in the past? The same way he'd been left? Squeezing her closer, he dropped a kiss on the top of her head. "No way."

Elodie took a big breath, releasing it slowly, clearly sinking back into dreamland. "They always leave me," he thought he heard her mumble. But wasn't sure he'd heard right.

He tensed all the same. Who had ever left her? Hurt her? He'd never do that. Not if she was his...

CHAPTER 10

"EAT..."

The voice in her head yanked her out of sleep in a cold sweat only to find the mist that surrounded her form when she became her monster now hovered over the bed.

The monster inside her was ravenous, and it would take Chance if it had no other option. On a gasp, she forced it back down. Deep. She needed to feed that side of her. Soon. Maybe she could find someone appropriate to dispatch and be back before Chance woke up?

No, the sun was starting to lighten the sky. She'd have to wait for night.

Not wanting to go back to sleep and risk losing control, Elodie managed to slip out of bed without waking Chance, who in slumber appeared even more angelic. She could see now where the cherub imagery came from. Not that he looked like a little boy. He was all man. But there was something sweet about him when he was relaxed this way.

Quickly, she dressed and went into the living room where she dug her phone out of her purse. A message notification caught her eye and she checked to find a note from Delilah.

. . .

CRETAN IN THE WIND. *Must have some magical help hiding or I would have found him. Lay low until I tell you it's safe.*

TERRIFIC.

She'd give Delilah until tonight, then she'd have to risk Cretan finding her. She'd just make him the meal.

Damn minotaurs.

She'd sucked the life out of Tavros, crushed his body into jelly, and fed on his aura. And now she had another bent on revenge. She was tempted to go to the gods to intervene. Sirens were off limits for other supernaturals to kill. But bringing gods in only made things messier. They weren't exactly predictable.

She glanced toward the bedroom where a sleeping god lay and did a mental revision. *Most* gods weren't predictable. Some were better than others.

A flash of memories—all from last night—crept over her along with an unsettling knowledge that she didn't want it to end.

Her stomach rumbled, though. It really sucked having both human and supernatural appetites, neither of which sated the other. However, she'd learned the hard way, ages ago, that she couldn't hunt on an empty stomach. Human hunger, or any kind of nagging discomfort really, made her monster harder to control.

So food first.

She set her phone to charging and moved into the kitchen, peeking through his cabinets. Chance really didn't cook for himself much, did he? Much like herself, actually. The fridge and cupboards were practically bare. At least he had some eggs—she checked the date—which were about to expire. Not enough for an omelet though.

"Pancakes it is."

Pulling her hair into a messy bun, she got to work,

humming to herself as she moved about the kitchen. She was at the stovetop, her back to the room, watching the first batch of pancakes cook on the griddle when a solid arm stole around her belly, pulling her up against a bare male chest. Disappointment that she hadn't gotten out of here fast enough warred with the need to lean back into him.

Chance drew his other hand up her yoga-pant covered thigh to her hip. He was still warm from sleep and smelled like pure male and sex.

"If you make me burn these pancakes, we'll have nothing to eat." She belied her words by leaning into him though.

Gods she was weak.

Nuzzling the side of her neck, he hummed an unconcerned sound, and the hand at her hip crept up to the waist band of her pants.

Her body was screaming *hell yes*, but her heart pounded at the thought of unleashing her monster on him, so swatted at the hand. "I mean it."

Chance chuckled, the sound more devil than angel. Why had she thought him sweet again? "I'm pretty sure we proved yesterday that I can make you come while you're...otherwise occupied in the kitchen."

With no more protest from her, those wicked fingers found their way further south, under the band of her panties, and she gasped when he brushed against that bundle of nerves that throbbed in the wake of his touch.

Maybe she could feed both these hungers before going out and feeding her siren side. The monster in her gave a low hum of agreement. Was it worth the risk?

If the mist appeared, she'd run.

Deliberately, she reached out and flipped a pancake. Then another. Matching his actions to hers, Chance rubbed and flicked her clit in time with each flip of a pancake. She was never going to look at pancakes the same way again. Just like tea. Too bad she couldn't just keep flipping and flipping and flipping until…

He slid a finger lower, up and into her, using his thumb to press at the spot he'd just been flicking. Eyes on the griddle, Elodie canted her hips to the rhythm of his pumping, already close to the edge. When he added two fingers, she moaned, trying to hold back the sensations that wanted to tumble loose.

He stopped his fingers and she moaned again. "Don't—"

"The pancakes are going to burn, love," he teased at her ear. "Better do something about that."

Oh, she was going to do something all right. She flipped those pancakes to a platter already sitting on the counter and turned off the heat.

"Who gave you permission to stop—"

He cut himself off as she twirled out of his arms, then, backing up as she kept her eyes on his, quickly discarded all of her clothes.

"Fuck me, Elodie," he muttered. And raised the hand he'd been using on her to suck his fingers while she watched.

Damned if that didn't send a new flash of heat through her, but Elodie wasn't a siren for nothing.

She hitched herself up onto his kitchen table and spread her legs wide, feet propped on two chairs that screeched a protest as she shoved them where she needed. Then, mimicking his actions, she sucked her own fingers and lowered them to touch herself.

Smiling as her happy-go-lucky cupid's expression changed to near feral, she put on a show. She worked her own body, watching him while he watched her.

And she was into it, heart and soul.

When he pulled his cock out of his pants, squeezing and flogging it violently, she almost came right then. Tossing her head back, she closed her eyes and imagined what he was seeing as she brought herself closer to that precipice. Hair wild, mouth open, moaning and writhing.

What she didn't picture was him scooping her right off the table to pin her against the wall and impale her on his cock in a single thrust, gravity helping him slide deep.

The instant she opened her eyes and met his gaze, she came. Hard.

Holding her gaze, Chance pounded into her, relentless, ruthless, and gods above, the possessiveness he was letting her see. She hated controlling men, but this was…different.

To her shock, another tingling warning took up at the base of her spine. Her only hint before another orgasm ripped through her.

"Fuck," Chance muttered in a strangled voice. Then, on a shout, he followed her over into bliss. Even so, he didn't stop fucking her until they both turned limp. Flipping them around, so that his back was to the wall, Chance slid down until he sat on the floor, her straddling him, his cock still buried inside her.

"The things you do to me."

"Well…I am a siren."

He tensed around her, then took her face in his hands, forcing her to look at him as he shook his head. "No. You're *you*."

She dropped her gaze, unable to handle the look in his eyes. The one that told her he meant that. "I thought I said no feelings," she whispered.

"Sorry," he whispered back. Disappointment surged despite her best intentions. Only then he buried a hand in her hair, massaging the nape of her neck, the move both comforting and possessive as hell. "But I never was one for rules."

Despite the happiness that buried that disappointment, or maybe because of it, she had no idea how to answer that. "Um…I guess I'd better finish our breakfast."

After a telling pause, he chuckled. "We keep getting inter-rupted when we try to eat."

"Yeah." She sat up straight, glancing around for something to help them clean up. "Next time, we should make the food part of the sex, so we get both."

His cock twitched inside her, thickening.

She widened her eyes at him, lips drawing up. "Already?"

Chance shrugged. "Don't talk about food and sex, because now I'm picturing what I could do with that."

Teasing, Elodie rolled her eyes. "Isn't that just like a man —" She cut off as the smell of smoke penetrated.

Smoke.

But she'd turned off the burner.

He must've smelled it too, because Chance levered them both up off the floor. "Something's burning."

Since he'd only lowered his jeans to fuck her, he just tugged them back up to check. She was halfway through getting herself dressed again—at this rate she should prob-ably give up and just spend her time here naked—when she caught his frowning search.

"What is it?"

"There's nothing here that's smoking."

She was right…she *had* turned off the stovetop.

"Did you leave your curling iron on in the bathroom?" he asked.

Elodie shook her head, even as part of her wanted to pause for a second and have a little moment where she could pretend they really were lovers, and not the temporary kind. The kind who lived in each other's pockets to such an extent that he would know she had a habit of forgetting to unplug her curling iron. "I haven't used it today."

"Then it's coming from somewhere else."

He stalked away, around the corner into the foyer. "Shit," she heard him mutter, and hurried after only to find smoke coming in under their front door in curling whisps.

Hand against the door, Chance turned a grim face her way. "It's already too hot to get to the stairs."

"I could call Delilah. She teleports."

He shook his head. "I have a way out."

Grabbing her by the hand, he tugged her out onto his balcony, then, with his hands in fists, he crossed his arms over his chest before jerking them down and out. In that instant, wings magically appeared at his back. Not white wings but glittering and golden, like his arrows, and just as ephemeral.

"I've never flown someone before," he warned as he scooped her up in his arms. "I hope to hells this works."

"What?" she might have screeched the word.

But it was too late. With a mighty flap, they shot up into the sky and over the edge of the balcony. He flew them down in circles until they reached the ground, not out front, but the back of the building in an alleyway. Already sirens of firetrucks could be heard around the other side.

Chance gave her an apologetic look. "My neighbor, Roger—"

"Go." She even shoved him a bit.

Clearly not liking having to leave her, he took back off into the skies. She shivered. Hard. Damn. New York was cold in February. Especially still in pajamas and no jacket or shoes.

"Every creature is afraid of fire," a menacing rumble of a voice sounded from behind her the instant Chance was out of sight. "Even gods apparently."

Technically, Hephaestus wasn't afraid of fire. Hades either. But she wasn't about to argue with a minotaur.

She turned slowly to face the man who was out for her blood and flinched. Not at the way he leaned against the brick wall of the building. Not at the way he was peeling an apple with a bowie knife either. But at his aura.

Nothing muddy about it now. Just pure evil intent.

CHAPTER 11

ELODIE SMILED. Deliberately.

Then opened her mouth…and sang.

Not a song that any man or god could write down and replicate. A siren's song was distinct to the listener. They heard whatever fit them best. Not even Elodie knew exactly what they heard, though some men had spoken descriptions out loud.

The most famous of which was Odysseus. After having his men tie him to the mast so he could listen, and stuff wax in their ears so they couldn't, he'd written about the experience. When he'd heard the words and the music, the song had enchanted Odysseus's heart. He longed to plunge into the waves and to swim to the island.

Elodie's own songs had never once failed her. So wonderful was a siren's musical talent that it was said they could even calm the winds. Which was true.

But Cretan didn't move by so much as a twitch. Didn't walk toward her spellbound, or fall to his knees weeping, or take out his cock and start fisting it as some men had been known to do when she sang.

Nothing. Not even a flicker of need crossed his face. How

was that possible? Or had he plugged his ears like Odysseus's men?

Regardless, she was still the bigger monster, even without the effect of her song. That was just the bait to make her victims pliable and draw them close. Fixing him in her sights, Elodie brought on the change. It was easy, with her monster already clawing to the surface.

"Your mistake," she said, as mist swirled around her. Her voice was no longer beautiful, coming out as a small girl screaming.

All pretense of being unconcerned fell away from Cretan to leave a man intent on her. But not in fear or defense. He was…

Is he studying me?

She halted the change before it hardly began. Not even a flash of lightning in the mist.

"Right," Cretan muttered, more to himself than her.

Narrowing her eyes, Elodie bent to grab a rock in the alley and threw it at him. Only the rock sailed through… nothing. It shattered the illusion, and what was essentially a holographic projection of the minotaur disappeared. He hadn't been there at all.

Magic. The word whispered through her. It was the only explanation. But how? Minotaurs didn't possess any magical abilities beyond their change in form.

Her monster in all her hunger and rage threw her head back and roared her frustration, mist and lightning going out from her in a shockwave. But Elodie, when she'd been chained to the ocean floor, had learned to cage the beast within her, a skill that served her now.

She forced her monster to remain inside, pushing her deep down where she couldn't emerge again easily. She would need to feed, and very soon. As soon as she could get away from Chance. She couldn't continue to risk his life like this. Or the lives of other innocents.

But…for now…she was back to herself.

"Um…your girlfriend has an amazing voice," a shocked voice sounded behind her.

She whirled to face Chance, his golden wings still visible as he stood beside his neighbor, who was staring at her like men stared at angels.

Elodie sighed. "Cover your ears," she said to Chance.

As soon as he did, she opened her mouth, singing again. Immediately Roger went dazed, slack-jawed and hazy-eyed. Her monster raged, because usually that was the sign of a kill, but Elodie managed to keep her shit together and closed her mouth.

Roger wouldn't remember a thing. Not Chance flying him out of a burning building or how he got to the ground and definitely not her singing.

"Let's go before he comes out of it."

Chance only took the time to get Roger to humans who could help him. Then he returned to Elodie and flew them away without question or hesitation.

CHAPTER 12

CHANCE PROWLED around Elodie's pristine white living room, staring out into the night and the quiet street where she lived, not thrilled to have ended up here a second time. He hadn't even wanted to come here the first time.

Everything had happened so fast, they hadn't gotten an opportunity to slow down until now.

She'd been a shivering ice cube of a woman almost as soon as their feet had left the ground. Sirens did better in Mediterranean environs, which was why so few made their homes in colder climates. Elodie was the only siren that he knew of to make her home in this city. After a heated argument, during which she'd only grown colder in his arms while he flew, he'd agreed to take her back to her place.

"We need to get out of the city," he'd said, already tipping his wings to leave the fastest direction out.

"No." Elodie's voice had held the kind of stubbornness he'd heard before. "My place."

"Hell no." Even now, he grimaced at the tension coiling in his muscles. "He has to know where you live," he'd argued.

"We'll have to take that risk. I need clothes."

Chance had scowled down into her beautiful, argumentative, upturned face. "What if he even wants you to go there? It could be a trap."

"I need clothes, and we need to regroup."

Chance had opened his mouth to argue but then she'd given a full body shiver, and it had finally penetrated his thick skull that she was risking exposure.

Fuck.

"I'll find you a warm place to hide and go get you clothes." Preferably out of the city, but even then, he hadn't thought she'd make it that far.

Then Elodie had laid her hand on his chest, the move so trustingly intimate that he actually held his breath. Those big brown eyes had been fathomlessly trusting on his, and he'd felt himself melting.

"My apartment is two minutes from here," she'd said quietly, reasonably. "And I'm a monster. If he comes, I can handle him."

Chance hadn't put up much of a fight after that. He'd shaken his head. Even standing here now, he still didn't like it.

"I'll be fast," she'd wheedled. "In an out."

Fuck. He blown out a harsh breath. "Gods save me from a determined siren."

Gods he was a sucker for her, just like every other male on the planet.

Once they'd gotten to her place, she'd showered to get some body heat going, then dressed. By the time she emerged, Delilah and Alasdair had teleported in to meet them.

After hearing the description of Cretan's holographic illusion, Delilah and Alasdair had exchanged a speaking glance only mates could share. One that said they had a pretty good idea of who was behind that particular issue.

A witch. Holograms were magic.

Which lined up with Elodie's first thought when she'd

seen it earlier. But the pair actually had an idea of a specific witch.

"Only so many witches associate with minotaurs," Delilah had said dryly.

True. Supernaturals tended to avoid the hotheaded, narcissistic creatures whose asshole setting was eleven on the dial.

Elodie had insisted on going with them to speak to the witch they suspected. And Chance insisted on going with Elodie, blaming the arrow's effects on his need to stay close to her. She'd side-eyed him but hadn't objected.

They hadn't found the witch though. Delilah had taken them several places to no avail, before finally returning them to Elodie's for the night. Which had set off another argument between Elodie and Chance with her insistence that being on her home turf gave them the advantage. The only reason he'd agreed to it was Delilah.

"I'll spell the apartment, so that nothing can get in," Delilah had offered. "But nothing can get out either."

"See." Elodie waved at her friend. "All settled."

There'd been something in her expression...something he couldn't pin down...that had sent unease into his belly, but there was no way to argue with both women. So he'd agreed.

And now here he stood. Waiting.

The spell involved going around to every window and door and locking them shut. Then Delilah had spelled it from the outside, not that he could tell. Elodie had said she needed to take another shower then, because she wasn't all the way warm and disappeared on him. He could still hear the sound of the running water, but it had been a while.

And Chance needed an outlet for all this unresolved energy.

He'd left Elodie on her own this morning to face the minotaur hunting her. What the fuck had he been thinking?

What if Cretan had actually been there? What if that damn bull had hurt her?

He stalked through her bedroom, frowning at her drawers thrown open and closet strewn with clothes. He knocked on the bathroom door, but no answer came.

"Elodie?"

Another knock. Another call. Still no answer.

What if she'd passed out or something in the shower? Hit her head? Anxiety added another layer to the fear and self-blame he was already wrestling with, turning to weight in his gut. Screw being a gentleman. He burst into the room to find the shower running…and the room empty.

"What the fuck?" He whirled and jerked to a halt at the sight of the small window, just the size for a petite woman like Elodie to fit through, wide open.

He ran to it and stuck his head outside, waving his arm around. Sure enough, Delilah's spell wasn't working on this, and the fire escape was right outside.

He jerked back into the apartment, smacking the back of his head as he did. "Damn it."

The trouble was he didn't know if she'd been taken or had gone out on her own. Either way, he had no idea where to even start looking. Which left him with only one option. Glaring at the offending window, he pulled out his cell phone and called Delilah.

"She's safe," she answered.

Relief huffed out of him on a sharp breath, but on the next inhale was replaced with anger. "What the fuck, Delilah?"

"She needed to feed."

Feed? He would have made her something to eat if she was hungry. "So you gave her an escape hatch?"

"She was worried about hurting you."

Which might have pulled him up short if he wasn't so damn pissed. "Where'd she go?"

"I have a tracker on her. She's safe. In fact, she's already marked her target."

Target?

Realization pierced his anger like an arrow through his chest. This was a different kind of hunger his siren was dealing with. One he couldn't help sate. Fuck. Of course. She'd been hunting when he'd shot them both with his arrow.

At least Elodie had bothered to get help so she could feed as safely as possible. But the fact that she felt as if she had to hide this from him... He thought they'd made more progress than that. That she trusted him. He shook his head, glaring at his reflection in the mirror. "What do I do?" he asked Delilah.

"Wait there. She'll be home soon."

"I hate waiting," he muttered.

Delilah's chuckle was genuinely amused. How could she be laughing right now? But when she spoke, she wasn't laughing. "When she gets home, she'll need two things, and two things only."

"Which are?"

"A shower and help getting to sleep. Sirens like Elodie— the rare few who feel guilt—don't sleep well after kills, even though the act drains them physically." Delilah paused. "Good luck," she said before hanging up.

After a beat, Chance slipped his phone into his pocket, turned off the water, then stood there, debating his next move. Listen to Delilah and wait, or try to find his siren somewhere in Manhattan?

Not exactly a choice.

∼

ELODIE DIDN'T KNOW what she expected when she returned home. The cynical part of her semi-expected Chance to be in the living room nursing a beer, oblivious to her disappearance. She'd managed to hunt and feed in under an hour after all. But she knew that wasn't the case when she found the shower turned off and the bathroom door busted open. He'd broken it off its hinges.

Not a good sign.

Taking a deep breath, she tried to will herself to meet the confrontation she knew was coming. A kill always left her strangely depleted, exhausted, and at the same time so wired she never could settle. But she owed Chance an apology.

She leaned around the door to peek into her room. "Chance?"

Her bedside light flicked on and Chance rose from where he'd been sitting on the edge of the bed. He stared at her unblinking for a long moment, and she found herself wishing that she could see his damn aura. Was he angry? Disappointed? Disgusted?

"That didn't take long," he finally said.

She hesitated.

"Delilah told me where you went. I called her."

Elodie winced. "I'm sorry. I didn't think you'd let me go alone otherwise."

"You're right." The growl in his voice and the way his hands were clenched at his sides…he was definitely angry. "I would have insisted on going with you."

Exactly what she'd been afraid of. She never wanted him to see her like that. Not ever. It would change the way he looked at her from then on.

Chance ran a hand through his hair, standing it up on end. "We'll talk about trusting me more tomorrow."

Elodie frowned. Was her exhausted mind hearing wrong? "And tonight?"

He searched her gaze. "Delilah said you'd want a shower and maybe some help getting to sleep. I can help with that much, at least."

Unexpected tears burned at the back of Elodie's eyes. "You want to help me sleep after I just killed a man?"

"Did he deserve it?"

An older man who apparently had a thing for teenaged girls. The younger the better. He'd seduce them, then discard them when he'd had his fill, often leaving them pregnant or their confidence so in tatters their relationships would never be whole after that. How many lives had he ruined before she stopped him? She didn't want to think about it. The important part was he was stopped.

"Yes."

"That's what I thought." Chance crossed the room and stepped over the door to crowd right into her space, taking her face in his hands. "The shower is to clean off his scent?"

Chance Eroson might just be her undoing. How could he have guessed that? "His everything."

He nodded. "How about we replace it with something better?"

Him. He didn't need to say it. She heard it just fine in his voice.

"I was thinking we might shower together." He grinned suddenly, every inch the irresistible charmer she'd first met. "I hear an orgasm is great to help a body unwind and find sleep. But only if it will help."

Usually when Elodie came home from a kill, she felt dirty and unworthy and wrong. She didn't want to see anyone else for days. Not until she'd showered a thousand times and finally slept soundly.

She had never, not once in her two hundred years, thought she'd smile after one. But she found herself doing just that, though it felt weary on her face. "It's certainly worth a try."

CHAPTER 13

THE CALL HAD COME in the middle of the night. Chance had taken it, telling Ellie to sleep. Delilah had tracked down the witch.

Which was how he found himself watching from the edge of a snowy clearing in the rolling mountains of Vermont as Elodie, bundled up this time at least, pretended to creep toward a small cabin.

The cabin itself was innocuous. Cozy even, with firelight flickering in the windows inviting a passerby in for warmth on such a cold night. Not that they'd get any passersby here in the middle of nowhere.

What was inside wasn't so innocent.

He glanced at Alasdair and Delilah, both positioned beside him, watching intently. They hadn't tracked the minotaur, but they had found the witch he'd been using. Cretan's lover, apparently. She was inside.

And Elodie was bait.

This was a stupid fucking plan.

"She's in there, but he isn't?" he whispered at Alasdair. "You're sure of it?"

The warlock nodded, not taking his eyes from Elodie and the cabin.

He'd barely finished the movement when, with no warning and only a stirring of the snow around her, two people appeared beside Elodie.

Two. Not one.

The witch and the minotaur both. Unmistakably, the man already shifted into his half-bull form. Every muscle in Chance's body went so tense he might as well have been turned to stone by Medusa. But the three of them didn't move. Elodie was supposed to change. Supposed to attack.

Except the monster inside her didn't emerge.

The minotaur shot out a hand, taking her roughly by the throat and lifting her up so that her feet dangled in the air. Kicking and struggling, Elodie wrestled with his hands. But the fucker only smiled at her efforts.

"Screw this…" Chance moved his hands in a fluid motion like he was drawing his bow. That was all he had to do to call it to him. Immediately, it manifested in his grip, already nocked and drawn.

This one wasn't golden though. Still glittering, it was gunmetal grey. The arrow was one of lead. He rarely used this kind. They weren't very fun to fire, but they were effective.

"What are you doing?" Delilah whisper-hissed at him.

"Taking away his love. The witch will be less likely to help him if she finds him abhorrent."

Alasdair flicked a glance his way. "Remind me not to piss off any cupids."

"It only works if the love is weak," Chance muttered through clenched teeth, taking careful aim.

"How do you know it is?"

"I don't. In fact, if it's an obsessive, Bonnie and Clyde style relationship, this won't do jack shit. But it's worth a try. If nothing happens, step in."

Alasdair nodded.

Without hesitation, he fired his arrow. The glittering gray shaft was silent and swift arching up before shooting back to earth.

Which was when things went…weird.

Time seemed to slow to a crawl all around him, even the breeze was slower, the rustle of a creature under the brush dragged out. And his arrow hung suspended in the air, barely moving.

The witch turned her head with agonizing slowness to connect with Chance's gaze across the field, despite his hiding spot.

Then her hands came up or started to, one aimed toward Elodie and one toward Cretan, who still held Elodie up, both of them strangely still and yet not. Again, the slow-motion effect lent an eerie, unreal, dreamlike quality to the action. Meanwhile, Chance was frozen in time. All movement was leaden, as if his mind was still operating at full speed, but nothing else was. He knew he tried to shout the word "No!" and tried to start running for Elodie. But he'd barely opened his mouth or lifted his foot.

Then, without warning, the slowing went away and everything sped back up to normal in a jolting rush. In simultaneous instant, three things happened…

The arrow pierced the witch's heart. Even from this distance Chance couldn't mistake the way she recoiled from the sight of Cretan—the arrow taking effect and aversion twisting her features.

But her spells were already released.

One spell struck the minotaur and he disappeared instantly.

The other spell struck Chance. There'd been no time to shout, let alone get out of the way. It hit in the center of his chest and blasted him backward about thirty feet to collide with a tree with a crack of his head.

Vaguely Chance was aware of dropping to the snowy ground and the scent of burning flesh before he passed out.

ELODIE'S MIND took a solid thirty seconds to catch up with what had just happened. After time seemed to slow and speed up, all she knew was that she was on the ground now and Cretan was gone. The witch had managed to shoot a flash of magic past Elodie into the clearing, as well as send Cretan away, protecting her lover, if only temporarily, while at the same time being struck by a glittering magical arrow.

Elodie stared at the woman, who now looked down at her chest as though expecting to see a bleeding wound there. But there was none.

"No," the young witch—and she was young, nineteen at the most—gasped around the word, covering her heart with her hand. "He couldn't." She looked up, right into Elodie's eyes, tears slipping down her cheeks. "I loved Cretan. I know I did. That shouldn't have worked."

What was she talking about?

But the memories finally righted themselves in her head and a detail finally struck.

Lead. Not gold. The arrow Chance had shot at the witch was to take away love, not give it.

Before she could move, Delilah was suddenly beside her. "I'll handle her. Chance is hurt," she said before grabbing Elodie's hand. They teleported in a beat of silence before reappearing in the woods where she'd left her friends standing only minutes ago, though it felt like an age.

Chance wasn't standing, though. He was on the ground, out cold.

A blackened scorch mark sat, still smoking, dead center of his chest, the putrid scent of charred flesh heavy on the air. Alasdair knelt over him, hands glowing as he murmured the words of a spell.

Elodie was on her hands and knees beside him before she even remembered deciding to move. Taking one of his cold, limp hands in hers, she rubbed it, watching what Alasdair was doing. Repairing the wound, apparently. Before her eyes the flesh turned from white with black edges to white with little pink dots inside. Then those dots spread, becoming new flesh. Layers and layers forming until the edges started turning the silvery pink of scar tissue.

Vaguely, she was aware of Delilah disappearing, then reappearing with the witch in tow.

"What happened?" Elodie asked her friend over her shoulder, not looking away from Chance. Willing him to open his eyes.

"She hit him with a lightning bolt," Delilah's voice wasn't grim. She was pissed. "I should have predicted it."

"You couldn't have known—"

"Yes. I could. But this pregnancy—"

"Not with what I can do with time," the young witch offered through her sniffles, seemingly apologetic.

Chance suddenly coughed, the sound racking his body before he took a long, grating breath and opened his eyes. Only he didn't look at Elodie. He looked at Alasdair. "Damn, that hurt," he rasped.

Elodie scowled. "That is not funny."

Chance pushed himself to sitting, still not looking at her. "I know."

Alasdair ignored them both, continuing to heal Chance until all the flesh was pink and new. Then he sat back on his haunches. "If you'd been any closer, this would have killed you, but the tree took the brunt."

Chance rubbed at the center of his chest and winced. "Lucky me."

"How can you joke about this?" Elodie snapped. Mostly

because the relief that he was okay was making her snippy. A new sensation for her. Both the relief for someone else and the irritable reaction.

He looked her in the eyes finally, and suddenly she knew.

The effect of his arrow was gone. For both of them.

CHAPTER 14

HE'D KNOWN.

Chance had known the second he'd been struck with his own arrow. Of course, he knew all the rules. Drawing of blood, of either party struck by the arrow, cancelled out all effects. Not a little blood, but a lot. Enough to kill a man, which was why he hadn't brought it up as an option when they'd first been struck.

He was damn lucky to have had a powerful warlock right there to keep him from dying. He hadn't really been joking when he'd said that. Also, yeah, he'd been stalling. Not wanting to know it was all over. He'd needed more time to win her, to convince her love was worth trying for.

He stared at Elodie, watching the comprehension dawn in her widening eyes.

"The connection is gone," she whispered. Not a question.

"Yes."

"I—" She shook her head once, then her expression blanked, concealing the rest of any reaction she might be feeling from him. "I see."

What did she mean by that?

Alasdair held out a hand and they both gained their feet,

Elodie rising at the same time. "We need to get inside where it's warm and figure out our next steps."

Inside the cabin, they looked around. While the fire was crackling cheerfully, and various oil lamps added a warm glow, and the place was neat and tidy, it also clearly wasn't lived in. The furniture was pretty basic. No food in the cupboards or fridge. No personal items of any kind.

"What is this place?" Delilah demanded of the young witch. They still didn't know her name.

She shrugged, expression turning petulant. "A safe house for Cretan's people when needed. I'd never been here until tonight."

Without his anti-love arrow, she probably wouldn't be talking. At least they had that.

"Why were you here?" Chance asked.

"I may not love him now." The glance she flicked in Chance's direction was both resentful and awed. "But I won't hurt him either."

"He didn't love you," Chance said, earning a scowl from the girl.

"How would you know?"

"I'm a cupid. A god of love. My arrow wouldn't have broken your connection unless the love was weak. But I can tell you, as long as I've been doing this, I've seen it all. He was pretending to love you. He needed your magic."

Out of the corner of his eye, he caught the way Elodie slowly turned her head his direction. Studying him.

"He needed my help to kill the siren who killed his brother," the witch spat, throwing an accusing finger Elodie's direction. "I know. He told me everything, and she deserves to die."

Elodie stiffened, but her answer was quiet. "His brother had killed twelve women by the time I came across him."

Chance jerked his gaze to her. She hadn't mentioned that part before. Twelve women? He shuddered.

So did the witch. "How do you know that?" she whispered.

The glance Elodie sent his way was wary before she answered. "If I put my hand over someone's heart and look deep into their eyes I can...compel them."

The moment flying and arguing. His heart turned to lead. He'd thought she was trusting him, but she'd just been compelling him?

"They confess things. It's how I make sure I'm killing someone who deserves it."

Another glance his direction. Inscrutable, but Chance was too disappointed to decipher it anyway.

"How did he kill them?" the witch asked, as if compelled by Elodie to know the worst. Or the truth at least.

"Tavros preferred to gut them with his horns. Got off on it too." Elodie wasn't pulling her punches. "And the aura around Cretan...if he hasn't done similar, it won't be long."

The witch blanched.

"Where did you send him?" Elodie asked, still speaking softly. Gently even. As if she commiserated with the young, foolish witch.

The witch who looked as if she might vomit at any second, skin turning sickly green. "I don't know. I just knew I had to get him safely away before that arrow hit me."

"Will he return here?"

A shrug answered that. The witch wasn't in on Cretan's entire plan.

"Did he need something here beyond a place to hide?" Chance prodded.

The witch's gaze lifted to the wall above Elodie's head where the upstairs loft started. A minotaur's horns were mounted there.

No way. Cretan wasn't that sick that he'd nail his own brother's horns to the wall. Was he?

"Are those Tavros's?" Delilah asked.

The witch nodded. "He wants to kill her with them."

Chance watched the blood drain from Elodie's face, and almost went to her, but the way she was holding herself so stiffly, he forced himself to give her space. Plus, the disappointment with her was still heavy over him.

"He'll definitely come back for those," Alasdair muttered.

"Agreed," Delilah said. "Elodie and Chance, you should wait here for him to return. My love, take this young witch where she needs to go while I see if I can track the spell."

The witch glanced between the couple as if finally bothering to take a good look at them, then stared harder at Alasdair. "You're not... I mean you can't be..."

"I am."

The witch went even whiter than Elodie had. "That's just my luck," she muttered.

Alasdair didn't comment as he took her by the arm, and without even a disturbance of air, teleported them elsewhere. Delilah nodded and disappeared a second later.

Leaving Chance alone with Elodie.

"I didn't compel you," she said.

He stared across the room at her. Did he believe her? Elodie had never been a liar, but he'd also given in to her arguments after she'd done that. She'd also shut down on him now, not giving him even a glimpse of her emotions.

Back to the way it had been before.

Looking away, she moved into the living room and dropped onto one of the couches, the slump to her shoulders defeated.

Fuck this.

He did believe her. And he wasn't letting her just walk out of his life. Not without a fight.

He sat right down beside her and tugged her into his side. "You don't have to," she said. "The arrow—"

"I want to."

She went still and silent in his arms, but she didn't pull away either or protest.

"How's your neck?" he asked.

"It'll be black and blue tomorrow, but I'll live."

He was going to fucking kill that bull shifter.

"How's your chest?" she asked softly.

He hadn't been thinking about the fact that there was a gaping hole in his jacket and shirt. He glanced down at scar tissue that looked a good year or two old. Experimentally, he poked at the skin. It felt strange, but not painful. "Remind me to find a warlock who needs a new best friend. They are damn handy to have around."

Elodie chuckled at that, though the sound was a little forced. "I thought you were dead."

Had that bothered her? Hurt her? Would she have cared? He wanted to ask, but they were still feeling their way through this post-arrow situation.

For humans, who didn't know they'd been struck, the transition was near seamless from lust and physical desire to something deeper. He had no idea how two supernaturals, one who'd been in lust and the other who hadn't given a shit to begin with, would end up.

Chance tucked Elodie's head onto his shoulder and rested his cheek against the silk of her hair. "I'll take first watch," he said. "You get some sleep. We both need to be ready when he comes back."

Elodie was silent long enough that he started counting her breaths while he waited to see if she would pull away, go somewhere else to sleep or—

She snuggled into him. "Wake me in a few hours, okay?"

The knot tied tight in his belly loosened a smidge. "Okay," he whispered back.

He thought she'd fallen asleep, until a good fifteen minutes later she started moving her hand. Only the lightest touch at first, moving up his abs to his chest and the scar there, exploring it gently. Maybe she had been worried?

She lifted her head to stare at the spot as she touched it. "I was so scared," she whispered, not looking up.

His entire body clenched in reaction. She'd been scared for him? After his second arrow. Please let that mean something. "You were?"

She bit her lip and nodded slowly.

"I have a confession to make."

The thump of his heart was so heavy, she couldn't miss it with her hand against his chest. Could she.

"What's that?"

"I saw your red journal."

Chance grinned. "Snooping, huh?"

"I love that you care."

Which chipped away at the lead that had coated his heart with her earlier confession about compelling people. "Did you get to the last page?" he asked, winding a lock of her hair around his finger.

He held his breath, waiting for the answer.

"No."

He let that breath out silently, not quite sure if he was disappointed or relieved that she hadn't uncovered that little secret.

"But I liked the book. It made me like you even more."

There went all his breath again, gone in a whoosh. "You like me."

"I've always liked you," she whispered.

Chance closed his eyes, praying to every god and fate that he wasn't wrong, that there was something real here for her.

Elodie's hand drifted lower again, tracing his body with her fingertips. Teasing. A different purpose in the touch. Every brush was an awakening, but slow, like she was giving him time to put a stop to it.

No way was he stopping this. He wanted her. But even

more, he wanted to give her the chance to initiate something between them when she wasn't being influenced by his arrow's magic. Wanting, real wanting, had to be involved, but he needed her to know that.

He grunted when she got to a spot on his side just over his lowest ribs.

A low, sexy-as-fuck chuckle hit him with another jolt to the heart. "Ticklish?" she asked in a voice gone husky and full of temptation and...tentativeness, as if she wasn't sure of his reaction. Which got his attention. His siren was never tentative.

"Nope," he denied.

Those wicked fingers moved unerringly to the spot, and no matter how he tried not to move or react, she still managed to make him twitch as she tickled. "A flaw," she teased. "Finally."

He huffed a laugh that turned into a strangled growl as she undid the button and zip of his jeans and slipped that questing hand underneath to wrap it around his already hard cock.

"You want a guy with flaws?" he asked. Though the last word came out on a groan as she tightened her grip.

"There's such a thing as too perfect," she whispered, then pumped her hand.

Chance groaned. "I'm not perfect."

"Good." She adjusted the way she was laid against him, looking him in the eyes as she slowly worked her hand up and down his throbbing shaft. "I'm not either."

Then she claimed his lips in a slow, drugging kiss.

No powers compelled either of them. Not his. Not hers. This was just them. Together. He just wanted her, and that's what she was giving him now.

Chance turned into her and swept a hand slowly up her side, testing her curves, memorizing her. Breathing her in.

"Chance?" she whispered against his mouth.

He gazed into her doe brown eyes. "What?"

"Will you make love to me?"

He almost smiled, because that's exactly what they were doing, but she was serious. What was she asking?

She let go of him and cupped his face with both hands. "Not just fucking. Making love." She hesitated. "I don't know what that feels like."

Holy hells.

"It feels exactly like this, Ellie." He feathered his lips along the line of her jaw.

He willed her to feel his love for her in every touch, every sweep of his hand, every glance. Slowly, holding his own raging desire in check, he kissed her and touched her, undressed them both. He worshiped every inch of her and adored the way she responded and the way she followed his lead, doing the same to him.

She was a dance of contradictions—soft touches, almost tentative, as if she was learning to love this way for the first time. But then she let go on a soft sigh, and her boldness became something between the siren he'd been treated to and the woman she hid from the world.

He didn't know what had released that woman, but damned if he was going to ask.

Rolling Elodie to her back, Chance settled between her thighs, positioning himself. But he didn't enter her right away. Instead, he twined their hands together, drawing her arms up above her head.

She looked back at him, gaze dreamy and totally open. It was almost his undoing, because his body demanded he claim her. Hard.

Instead, he took his time, working into her in slow glides, teasing her, stretching out the anticipation and enjoyment for them both, and never looking away.

Because he wanted her to see him. To know this meant something to him.

Gradually he increased the pace, Elodie undulating with him, canting her hips. Every gasp, every moan from her lips went straight to his heart. When completion came over her, it came softly at first, with a beautiful kind of wonder in her eyes as wave after wave of pleasure crested through her, drawing him into his own explosive orgasm.

He didn't slow until they'd both wrung every ounce of pleasure from their bodies, then collapsed over her, burying his head in her neck, breathing her in, reveling in the sensation of being connected to her so intimately.

And entirely because she'd chosen it. No arrow involved.

Had chosen *him*.

He placed a kiss to the hollow behind her ear and smiled when she hummed her approval, but when he lifted his head to aim that smile at her, he froze.

Silent tears trickled down her cheeks.

Chance had never once felt panic that he'd hurt a partner. He considered himself a sensitive lover, doing his best to be attuned to her reactions and needs.

For that reason everything inside him turned sluggish. How was he supposed to respond? Ask her what was wrong? Give her space?

Before he could land on an answer, she smiled, and combined with the tears, the expression was like watching the first rays of sunlight hit frost on a field. Pristine and heavenly and quietly perfect.

"I didn't know it could be that way," she whispered.

She'd managed to crack his heart wide open. All these centuries and she didn't know? Had she only seen the worst of relationships, of people, only known the seedy or the violent?

Chance brushed her tears away with his fingertips, then gave her a soft kiss. "That's how it would always be between you and me."

CHAPTER 15

ELODIE COULDN'T REMEMBER a time when she'd ever woken so completely contented. Chance was with her, his arm wrapped around her stomach, holding her against him. And she was…

The feelings were real.

Maybe the arrow's magic didn't force unnatural, unlikely, or even unwanted feelings on someone. It was that it amplified whatever feelings were there. For her, starting with a strong chemistry, but eventually working its way down to the heart she'd thought was frozen long ago.

Because the power of Chance's arrow had been broken, and nothing had changed for her. She still wanted him. More than that, she *cherished* him.

Chance Eroson was a good, strong, kind man who believed in love, gave humanity a little more credit than they deserved, and filled her with the kind of hope she'd felt only as a young siren. Before what she witnessed regularly knocked it out of her.

And all of that only made her want to love him harder.

Love him.

I love him.

She didn't bother asking herself when that had happened. She had a feeling it had started long before that golden arrow had shot through her.

But if she loved him, she owed it to him to show him exactly who she was. Including the monster. He had a right to know, to have all the facts before…

"Chance—"

A massive boom reverberated around the cabin, shaking the bed.

What in the seven hells? She scooped the sheet around her and ran to a window to find not only Cretan standing in the field, but he'd brought friends. Ten minotaurs altogether, already shifted into their half bull-half man forms.

Chance was at her side almost as fast, already pulling on his pants.

Elodie spun and raced for her clothes, dressing in record time, but he beat her to the door just the same. "Stay here and call Delilah. I'll keep them busy."

She put her hand over his on the doorknob, keeping him from opening it. "You know I have a better chance of fending them off."

He shook his head, visibly reluctant to send her into danger—a siren was a monster, but against ten minotaurs even she would be tested.

Elodie softened. "I love that you want to keep me safe."

His jaw worked under her touch and he closed his eyes. "Go." He jerked the door open for her.

"Whatever you do, don't listen," she warned him.

As regal as any royal, Elodie walked out with her head held high. Rather than bother with some stalling monologue, she opened her mouth and sang.

And nothing happened.

Cretan smiled, though the expression was closer to a sneer. "You can learn a lot from legends," he said. "Even though they got the story of the minotaur's defeat of Theseus all wrong, Odysseus having his men stuff their ears with wax to not fall under the spell of sirens...brilliant move."

None of them could hear her song then. She couldn't draw them closer to compel them. Terrific.

That left Elodie with only one option. Let her monster loose and dare them to come close.

THE SECOND MIST started to form around Elodie, Chance knew what she was about to do. Delilah was coming. She should be here any minute, but no way was he letting the love of his long life face down ten minotaurs on her own.

Before she could finish her change, he burst from the cabin, drawing his bow as he did. "Hold your human form," he yelled.

Then he started shooting.

Golden arrows this time. Not lead.

Every one of those beasts were about to fall in love with a siren. Even unable to hear her song, Elodie was too beautiful for these creatures to not to have already felt at least a stirring of lust. Hopefully enough to make them hesitate to attack her now.

Usually, he got a chance to line up, make sure his aim was true so that the arrow struck both the people he was aiming to help find love in one shot. But Chance's uncle was the god of war, and a cousin was the goddess of the hunt. He'd been well trained with his weapon. In rapid fire succession, he shot and shot and shot. And his aim was true.

Never once striking Elodie, his arrows hit each minotaur with satisfying accuracy, straight through the heart, every single one. His arrows were silent, but he imagined the thunk of each strike. What he failed to do, though, was pay attention to their leader. As he turned his back on the love-struck creatures to his right to aim for those on the left, Cretan charged.

The minotaur's roar was nothing to the thunder of his hooves as he pounded across the icy field. Chance had never seen one in action before. He'd heard of their power, their strength. Near undefeatable. What no one had warned him about was their speed.

Only Hermes, made faster by his winged shoes, could have kept up. Chance hardly had time to blink before the thing was on him.

Except an obsidian tentacle knocked him out of the charging bull's path.

CHAPTER 16

DRAGONS SHIFTERS CHANGED shape with a shimmer. Wolf shifters in the blink of an eye, too fast to discern the process. Werewolves rearranged their bones. But sirens…

Sirens unleashed.

In a violent swirl of mist and electric charge that looked like lightning, Elodie burst from her skin into her true form.

Not a mermaid exactly. Not anymore.

Her grandmother on her rock near Scylla looked more mermaid than Elodie did. But the sirens were devoted to Persephone and had begged for wings to search for her when she'd been abducted by Hades. Demeter, in her mother's need to save her child, had granted them that wish.

Elodie's skin turned to scales obsidian dark, her eyes to slitted red irises with nictating membranes, her fingers and toes to webbed talons to both swim and rend flesh from bone, her teeth sharpened to rows in her mouth like a shark. She stood on feathered legs with an octopus's tentacles flowing from her center, already seeking her prey. And from her more human arms, great feathered wings emerged, black as a raven. Only her hair remained the white blonde of her human form.

Rather than flinch or run or faint—most fainted when they saw her this way—Cretan turned his rage from Chance to her.

The minotaurs whom Chance's arrows struck, stared at her in awe. One or two started to move toward her as though they might protect her. The ones whom Chance hadn't hit roared their own challenge, but the sound cut off abruptly as more arrows flew, striking each in turn.

Elodie's monster smiled. Good.

Cretan charged, but she lashed out with her tentacles, sweeping his legs out from under him. Both stalking and slithering forward. Using both her legs and tentacles, she stopped when he regained his feet and charged again.

Damn he was fast.

She couldn't let him strike her. At that speed, lowering his head and using his horns, he would either impale her or pulverize whatever he hit.

But she didn't move. Instead, the mist swirled and lightning flashed and she grew in height and form until she towered over him. At this size, his charge would be merely a sting.

Unswayed by her massiveness, Cretan struck with all his force. She took the hit in a leg and the reverberation of it traveled through her entire body, toppling her over. Elodie groaned in pain.

"Elodie!" Chance's yell reached her, focusing her.

Cretan hit with the force of a god. No wonder this creature had been so feared.

Spreading her wings wide, she took to the air. Not to escape, but to give herself a chance to return to normal size. Bigger wasn't going to work.

Only one thing would. She needed to draw him close, but before he got a full head of steam under him.

Deliberately, as her perspective neared the ground, Elodie fell to her side, clutching at her leg. She allowed her tentacles to writhe and flop around herself, spraying snow into the air. She hoped to hells she appeared lamed and vulnerable.

"Elodie!" Chance's yell sounded louder from down here.

To her horror, he started to run for her, her act obviously too good. Only if she signaled him to stay away, Cretan would see.

The minotaur put on a burst of speed and beat him to her. Only instead of ramming her, he screeched to a halt at her side, casting her in shadow, his smile a gloating sneer on fleshy animal lips.

"Is this how my brother looked?" he asked. "Pathetic and crawling on the ground, desperate to get to you, called by your song. Before you killed him in cold blood?"

"No," she said in that childlike scream of a voice, only beautiful in song. "*This* is how he looked."

A single wriggling tentacle wrapped around his leg. The suction and muscle of it impossible to escape. With a yank she pulled him into her, the rest of her tentacles wrapping around him. Cretan's eyes bulged in shock as he toppled over. Then he yelled, jerking and clawing to get away from her, but once a man was this near, there was no escaping.

The monster was in full control now, tentacles crushing him while dragging him ever closer. She spread her wings wide and opened her terrible maw, showing him dagger-like teeth. Her monster liked them afraid.

With an unearthly sound, she pulled him up against her and sank her teeth in his neck, rending flesh from bone.

Cretan screamed and thrashed until she bled him dry. Until a final death rattle shook his body and his eyes went glossy, rolling back in his head.

The monster had fed recently though.

Rather than fall on him like the rabid animal, she was satisfied with his death. She dropped his limp, still draining form to the ground where she stood in a spray of red blood over the white snow.

Chest heaving, she looked across the field. To Chance.

He'd stopped running to her, probably when she attacked the minotaur. Now he stood, watching her with an expression that was...nothing. Total blank. Hiding his thoughts from her. His disgust, no doubt.

A lance of pain speared through the hope that still lingered after last night.

Delilah and Alasdair appeared beside Chance suddenly. A little too late. Only Chance didn't look away from her.

Closing her eyes, Elodie brought about the change, the glow of the lightning in her mist lighting up her eyelids in flashes. But when she opened her eyes, Chance wasn't there anymore.

That metaphorical lance of pain plunged through her heart. Impaling her.

"Where'd he go?" she forced herself to ask as Delilah moved closer.

Her friend shook her head. "We don't know. He just... disappeared. I've never seen someone disappear that fast."

Some gods could do that, she was aware. But Chance had wings. Why would he need that ability too?

Does it matter? He's gone.

Like others before him, he'd taken one look at what she became, what she could do, and he couldn't stomach it.

He was gone, taking her shattered, bleeding heart along with him.

CHAPTER 17

ELODIE SAT on the couch in her apartment in a state. Pajamas, unwashed hair, food containers from takeout littering the room. She couldn't make herself lie in the bed. Not where he'd held her so sweetly after her previous kill. At least she wasn't in the cabin where they'd made love. This…what they'd done here had just been fucking.

Liar, a tiny voice in her head whispered.

She was starting to hate that inner voice.

Elodie hadn't been out since she'd gotten home, and even though tonight—Valentine's Day—was one of her best hunting nights, seeing all those couples celebrating their love…she didn't feel up to facing that. She'd feed in another day or two when the hubbub of the holiday had died down.

At least she was no longer being stalked by a vengeful minotaur. Delilah and Alasdair had unspelled Cretan's pals from Chance's arrows, then taken them back to their people for punishment, which she hoped was being handled right. She was too heart weary to check in. Delilah would tell her if something went awry. Elodie needed to be alone.

And no one noticed. She hadn't shown up anywhere, talked to anyone, and no one had noticed.

The thought made her tense and then sit up straighter, letting go of her knees.

What am I doing? In all her years she'd been bitter, jaded, disgusted even. When previous lovers had left her, she'd been heart sore, but not broken. What she had never been, though, not once, was defeatist.

Damned if she was going to let herself become that now.

It was Valentine's Day. If there was ever a day to lay all her cards on the table, declare her love, and let the chips fall where they may—which was probably too many idioms— this was the day. If Chance had taught her anything, it was that hope and love were both worth fighting for.

Elodie jumped up and headed into her room, where she pulled out a dress worthy of the classy woman she was and started getting herself ready to knock Chance Eroson's socks off.

Another idiom. Apparently, courage meant thinking in cliches.

An hour later, she applied the last touch to her makeup, then stepped back from the mirror to check out the finished effect. This wasn't the siren. This was her. Entirely her.

The dress was understated, navy with a slim, sleeveless top and flaring skirt, but cut so beautifully it showed off her curves and made her feel sexy while being nothing like the over-the-top dresses she wore when hunting. Her white-blond hair she'd pulled into a simple ponytail. Makeup also understated.

This was the woman she wished men saw when they looked at her. Who she'd hoped Chance saw. This wasn't the casual version of her, but Chance had already seen that version.

A knock at her door made her jump.

She wasn't expecting anyone. With a frown, she went through to the foyer and checked the peep hole, then hurried to open the door. "Delilah? Did something go wrong with—"

A gentle hand on her arm stopped the worries spilling out of her mouth. "Nothing's gone wrong. Cretan was acting without the consent of the bull shifter's leaders. This is over. No one will come after her again.

"Oh. Okay." That was a relief at least. Elodie stepped back to let her friend in. "You could have called. You didn't have to come all this way just to tell me that."

"I didn't." Delilah eyed her up and down. "I came to tell you to stop hiding and go talk to Chance. He's back in town tonight."

He hadn't been home? It had been days now. Where had he gone? She'd just assumed when he hadn't called or gotten in touch or showed up—

Turning away she grabbed her matching coat and hand-bag. "I don't mean to be rude, but I have to go see Chance."

"Then turn around and look."

Suddenly popping up in front of her, Delilah smiled, then disappeared.

On a gasp, Elodie whirled to find Chance standing in her hallway. Despite the cocky grin, there was an uncertainty in his eyes that made her heart soar. That and the bouquet of roses clutched in his hand.

"Chance," she breathed, then launched herself at him.

He caught her against his chest with a grunt, one arm wrapping around her tightly as she buried her face in his neck. "Whoa." He chuckled. "Now that's the kind of greeting I could get used to."

"I thought you left because you were horrified."

He sighed. "My father summoned me home to Olympus to explain. He did it so fast, and your eyes were closed, so I didn't get the chance to warn you."

He was right. He'd been there. She'd closed her eyes. And when she'd opened them, he was gone. Definitely no time. But why had he been summoned?

"Explain?" She pulled back to see his face. And what she

found there was regret and worry and that hope she loved so much about him.

"I've never had to let loose so many arrows at once," he said. "They're precious, formed by Hephaestus for my kind, and imbued with my father's power. He feels it leave him every time one is used. He wanted an explanation."

"Oh."

Chance bent a serious look on her, arm tightening around her. "I would *never* be horrified by any part of you. You were…"

She held her breath waiting for she didn't know what.

"Amazing. You *are* amazing."

His deep rumbled assurance unleashed a relief so deep tears sprang to her eyes. She didn't care. "I fell in love with you and I was so scared you didn't feel—"

"Whoa." Hands at her shoulders pulled her away and he stared at her tears first with shock, then a growing wonder. "You mean it?"

Elodie sniffed. "That I love you?"

He nodded slowly.

"I was just coming to find you to tell you and hope maybe —" For the first time in her entire life, Elodie turned shy. Tongue-tied even.

"Maybe I love you too?" He smoothed the tears from her cheeks, but his smile was what healed the last wound in her heart. "I do. I have for a long time."

He let her go and, with a gesture of his hands and a sparkling of gold, was suddenly holding the red leather-bound book. He flipped to the last page and showed her…"

No pictures. Just their names entwined. "I wanted our story to be in here," he said.

Gods. He really had loved her all this time? She traced the letters which were red for his name and gold for hers. Gold, like the glitter of his magic. Did the think of her as magical, because she definitely thought of him that way.

"It's why my arrow worked on us."

She blinked and lifted her gaze from the book. "Worked?"

Chance's grin was maybe the most beautiful thing she'd ever seen. "My arrows don't force feelings that aren't already there. They only enhance what is. It's not a deception—it's more like getting inhibitions out of the way."

"Like fast-forwarding to the good part," she whispered.

"Exactly."

Her lungs tightened, but the sensation was a sort of giddy happiness, and she smiled. "So is this the good part?"

Disappearing the book in another glitter of gold, he pulled her close again and kissed her lips in a slow, deliberate claiming. Both sweet and possessive. "This is the beginning of the good part for us," he murmured against her.

Elodie sank into him, even as she battled a few of her remaining worries. "I'm still a siren. I have to feed."

"I know. We'll figure it out."

She believed him. What's more…she trusted him and the risk. If things did end down the road, even this small moment of happiness now was worth it. Just to feel the way she did in his arms. Even if it didn't last. But she sure as hells hoped it lasted.

"So you were coming to get me?" he asked.

She nodded. "I was going to take you on a Valentine's date."

He grinned. "Really? What kind of date?"

"Anything you want."

The twinkle in his eyes turned mischievous. "Anything?"

She nodded, undaunted.

"In that case…" He parted his shirt, superman style, to show her a silky red shirt underneath.

She lifted her brows. "Um…"

"I brought you a pair, too."

A pair of what?

He leaned over and pulled a wrapped box from a pile of

bags in the hallway that she hadn't noticed until now. Casting him a bemused glance, still not quite able to believe this was real, she opened the gift to find…pajamas. Red silk pajamas that she assumed matched the ones he was wearing under his suit. She eyed the other items on the floor. "Takeout?"

Chance's grin widened. "A few different kinds. And I'll set up my streaming so we have lots of romance movies to pick from."

"Only the good parts though?"

He grinned. "And three different kinds of chocolates for eating in front of the fire."

Everything she'd said she wanted.

He picked up the roses he'd dropped at some point during their reunion. "But I'm cupid. I had to bring the flowers, too."

On a delighted laugh, she took them and inhaled deeply. "I love them."

"Loves roses. Noted." He pretended to write that down in a notebook and she laughed.

"Likes to tease. Noted." She did the same. Then held out a hand. "Be my Valentine?"

"I thought you'd never ask." He tugged that hand and pulled her into him, kissing her soundly. "I think I've loved you since the day we met and you told me to shove my arrows up my—"

"I'm glad you didn't take that advice. It's a very nice backside."

"Come on. Let's eat before the food gets cold. Then maybe I'll let you appreciate my ass without clothes on." He waggled his eyebrows suggestively.

Elodie laughed as she bent down to scoop up bags of takeout. She'd done that—laughing—more with him than she had in at least the last decade. "Maybe I'll let you appreciate mine."

Chance groaned as she let him get a good look right that

moment. "I can see life with a siren is never going to be boring."

Life with a siren. An indefinite state of things she hoped might last forever, starting with tonight.

"A siren who lures men to their deaths and a cupid who helps humans fall in love. Who could ever have predicted our falling for each other?"

"Well…." Chance drew out the word like he'd known all along. He always did like the odd pairings.

Following her inside, he plopped the food down and pulled her in for another kiss. "I definitely owe the fates for their hand in this."

She sighed into him and for the first time in a long, long time, looked forward to her future, to seeing where her life would lead with Chance at her side.

"Happy Valentine's Day, Ellie."

For maybe the first time ever, she didn't roll her eyes, instead, embracing his meaning for the day. "You too, my love. You too."

ALSO BY ABIGAIL OWEN

Don't miss the Brimstone Inc. series...
THE DEMIGOD COMPLEX
SHIFT OUT OF LUCK
A GHOST OF A CHANCE
BAIT N' WITCH
TRY AS I SMITE
HIT BY THE CUPID STICK

Brimstone Inc. is set in the same world as...
INFERNO RISING
FIRE'S EDGE

Abigail also writes as...
Kadie Scott | steamy contemporary romance
Kristen McKanagh | sweet contemporary romance

ACKNOWLEDGMENTS

Dear Reader,

Writing and publishing a book doesn't happen without the support and help from a host of incredible people.

To my fantastic paranormal romance readers... Thanks for going on these journeys with me, for your kindness, your support, and generally being awesome. The second I mentioned a Cupid and a Siren at the end of Try As I Smite I knew this needed to be a Valentine's Day story. I hope the wait for Chance and Elodie was worth it. They were a lot of fun to write! If you have a free sec, please think about leaving a review. Also, I love to connect with my readers, so I hope you'll drop a line and say "Howdy" on any of my social media!

To my beta readers Nicki, Kait, Latoya, Melissa, Luise, Guadalupe, and Sierra...your feedback made this a better story!

To my team of friends, sprinting partners, beta readers, critique partners, writing buddies, reviewers, and family (you know who you are)... I know I say this every time, but I mean it... Your friendships and feedback and support mean the world to me.

Finally, to my husband...I love you so much. And to our awesome kids, I don't know how it's possible, but I love you more every day. I can't wait to see the story of your own lives.

Xoxo, Abigail Owen

ABOUT THE AUTHOR

Multi-award-winning author, Abigail Owen, writes paranormal romance & upper YA/new adult fantasy romance. She loves plots that move hot and fast, feisty heroines with sass, heroes with heart, a dash of snark, and oodles of HEAs! Other titles include wife, mother, Star Wars geek, ex-competitive skydiver, spreadsheet lover, eMBA, organizational guru, Texan, Aggie, and chocoholic.

Abigail grew up consuming books and exploring the world through her writing. She attempted to find a practical career related to her favorite pastime by earning a degree in English Rhetoric (Technical Writing) and an MBA. However, she swiftly discovered that writing without imagination is not nearly as fun as writing with it.

Abigail currently resides in Austin, Texas, with her own swoon-worthy hero, their (mostly) angelic kids, who are growing up way too fast, and two adorable fur babies.

http://www.abigailowen.com

facebook.com/Abigail.Owen.Books
twitter.com/AOwenBooks
instagram.com/abigailowenauthor
bookbub.com/authors/abigail-owen

Made in the USA
Columbia, SC
30 January 2022

55001111R00063